Happy Times Too
A Novella
J.B. Lee

J.B. Lee

Author's Note

Thank you for taking a chance on Happy Times Too!

This book follows Paul Gunter, who is introduced in *Falling Apart Together*, and while reading that book will help you better understand his character, it is not necessary to read before this novella. This story is, at its core, about finding love after losing the one you thought you would spend your forever with.

For those who like to know when the spice happens, there is a dicktionary located at the back of the book.

As much as I'd love for you to read this book and fall in love with these characters, your mental health matters. This book contains the following topics, and if you don't feel like you can read this, please do not hesitate to put it down and find something more lighthearted.

Content Warnings:
Grief
Loss of Spouse (cancer and car accident)
Seizures, on Page (epilepsy)

Brief Mention of Miscarriage
Brief Mention of C-Section/Hysterectomy, and Alludes
to Traumatic Birth
Hospitalization in Flashback
Explicit Sexual Content

This is not necessarily a list of songs to listen to while you read, but are songs I listened to while writing, or inspired certain scenes.

"Endless Love" by Diana Ross and Lionel Richie
"If Heaven Wasn't so Far Away" by Justin Moore
"Visiting Hours" by Ed Sheeran
"Beat You There" by Will Dempsey
"Leave A Light On" by Papa Roach and Carrie Underwood
"Beautiful Things" by Benson Boone
"I Wanna Sex You Up" by Color Me Badd
"Kiss the Sky" by Maren Morris
"In the Stars" by Benson Boone
"Save You a Seat" by Alex Warren
"My Girl" by The Temptations
"He Gets That From Me" by Reba
"Abracadabra" by Lady Gaga
"Golden" by KPop Demon Hunters
"A Thousand Years" by Christina Perri

To those who have loved and lost, it's okay to open your heart back up and love again.

Contents

Prologue
Paul

Two years ago . . .

Sherri has been withering away in front of my eyes for the past few weeks. My heart breaks with each ragged breath she struggles to complete and each coughing attack that erupts from her fragile body. Holding her hand, I absentmindedly rub her forearm while she rests.

I can feel her slipping away from us more each day and it feels like I'm not far from following behind her. Glancing over at the couch, I see Tessa rotate in her sleep. She's refused to sleep in her bedroom since Sherri started at-home hospice.

"Why are you watching me sleep, you weirdo?" Sherri whisper-laughs, her eyes still closed.

I squeeze her hand, chuckling. "And how do you know I'm watching you? I could be watching Tessa."

My wife opens her beautiful brown eyes, giving me a knowing look. I was definitely watching her sleep. "What's on your mind, Pauly?" She shifts on her bed to better face me.

"I was just thinking that I'm not ready for you to leave us," I answer honestly, tears coating my eyes.

She nods her head weakly. "I know, and neither is Tessa. But my body is ready—*I'm* ready. I just need a few things first." Her intense gaze never leaves mine.

"Anything, baby. Anything. What do you need?" I lean closer so I can hear her soft voice.

Turning her head, she lifts a hand to cover a cough. "First thing, don't forget those letters I gave you. They should be in the top drawer of my dresser." She leans forward to take a sip of the water I hold up for her. "Second thing, and this one I need you to *really* listen to." Her eyes narrow, making sure she has my full attention. "You promise me that, after God calls me home, you will find someone else to spend your life with. You are too young, too handsome, and too damn good-hearted to be lonely forever."

I try to swallow the lump that's formed in my throat. When I don't respond, she gives me her best teacher look and says, "Paul Gunter, promise me. Just because my life is ending doesn't mean yours has to too."

Chapter 1

Paul

Pulling into the parking lot of the community center, I put my truck in park. Leaning over, I reach into my glove box and grab my wallet, pulling out the well-worn envelope I keep with me. I unfold the letter for the third time today, rereading my wife's words. The same words she spoke to me during her last week on this earth.

My dear sweet Paul,

You've been my best friend, my partner in crime, my co-parent, and my soulmate for over half my life. But now, I'm unfortunately leaving you with a terrible new title. My widower. For that, I am forever sorry.

I can see how my diagnosis has wrecked you. You try to hide your emotions when I'm looking, but you forget how long I've known you. You've been my rock through this whole shitty situation and I'm forever grateful to have had you to call my husband for the past thirty-four years.

Pauly, I want you to promise me something. When the cancer has done its job and God has called me home, promise me you will find love again. Don't let the rest of your life pass you by alone. I *know it was our future that we spent years dreaming of, but now it's <u>your</u> future.*

Find someone who has the same kind heart as you—someone who will love Tessa even though she's not the one to have given birth to her. Find someone to laugh with and who isn't afraid to laugh at themselves—Lord knows I've laughed at myself more times than I can count. Be with someone who continues to challenge you and encourages you to chase your dreams of becoming Chief of Police. I know it'll happen! Find someone who believes it too. You're the one person who always kept me grounded, and I want you to find someone who can return the favor and ground you.

Promise me you'll find someone to share your happiness with. And please, Honey, always remember that I love you so much, but I know that you still have so much love to give. Fifty-three is too young to be losing your person, so don't close yourself off from loving again.

I will wait for you by Heaven's gate, my love.

I love you for eternity,

Sherri

Taking a deep breath, I run my finger along the side of the letter. "I can't believe it's been two years today, baby," I say to my wife's memory. "It feels like just last night I was holding you in my arms while we slow danced at our wedding." Blinking back tears, I refold the paper, returning it to its envelope.

"It is my honor to announce the new, Mr. and Mrs. Paul Gunter! If everyone wants to turn their attention to the dance

floor as Paul and Sherri make their way to the center for their first dance as husband and wife . . ." the emcee says into a microphone as we make our way to the middle of the floor.

Sherri looks radiant in her wedding gown—white lace sleeves, and matching lace flowing to the ground around her legs. She places her left hand on my shoulder and I hold my left hand up as she reaches her right one out. We slowly start to sway back and forth as "Endless Love" by Lionel Richie and Diana Ross plays.

"You are so handsome." Her eyes shine as she smiles at me. "I can't believe we're married! I'm looking forward to the life we'll create together."

As the song ends I dip her, locking our lips in a kiss, causing the crowd to erupt with cheers. "I love you so much, Sherri."

I look around the parking lot and see the familiar faces of other members of the Lost Love Grief Group—a group designed for widows and widowers. My therapist suggested I join after Sherri passed, and I've been coming weekly since losing her . . . give or take a week here and there.

Stepping out of my truck, I notice Gwen pulling into the spot next to me. A small smile creeps across my face when she glances my way.

"Hey, Paul!" She beams out her window as she parks her van.

I tug on my shirt in an unexpected nervous gesture as I stand at the hood of my truck, waiting for her to get out of her car. Gwen and her son moved to Middleburg a couple of weeks after Sherri died, looking for a fresh start of their own. Learning her story when she shared it in group was heartbreaking. But then again, everyone who comes here has a heartbreaking story.

"Hey, Gwen, how're you today?" I ask once she's next to me. She sweeps a lock of blonde hair behind her right ear, revealing a small purple ribbon tattoo.

Her blue eyes twinkle as she looks up at me. "Can't really complain too much today. Max seems to be having a good day and he felt comfortable enough with me leaving him alone so I wouldn't miss the meeting."

Once we've made it inside, Gwen goes to the table where they keep coffee and snacks and reaches for a cup. I already had coffee this morning, but even if I hadn't, I would have passed anyway. The coffee here tastes like dirt. Taking a seat next to Ian, I ask, "Hey, buddy, how are you doing?" patting him on his shoulder.

Ian lost his wife a few weeks ago and is new to the group so I've tried to make a point to befriend him. He's only twenty-three—they were newlyweds. His young age mixed with the fact that he was freshly married hits close to home with my daughter being a newlywed herself.

"I'm here. That's about as good as it's been lately," he responds as Gwen takes the seat on his other side.

I nod in understanding. "I get it. Sometimes getting out of bed and out of the house can make all the difference in your mood for the day. I'm happy you made it today."

Chapter 2

Gwen

I risk taking a glance at Paul as he converses with Ian. There's something about the way he carries himself that draws me in. His bald head shines under the fluorescent lights in this meeting room, and his blue eyes sparkle as he comforts his friend, evidence of a happy life showing in the lines on his face as he speaks.

Paul is always the first one to give a warm welcome to the newbies here at LLGG. I don't know what in particular made him take on that role when he isn't the one in charge, but it's definitely an endearing quality—one that has softened my heart toward him.

He was the first person to greet me in the parking lot on my first day, making this a little less overwhelming. If I'm being honest, he was my first friend here in Middleburg after Max and I moved. My co-workers are nice enough, but I was still in a state of shock when I first arrived and I didn't go out of my way to interact with anyone outside of work-related tasks. Plus, having a son who had just been diagnosed with epilepsy wasn't conducive for me going out and mingling.

I'm broken out of my trance when I hear Gayle, the coordinator, call the meeting to a start. "Good morning, everyone. I'm so glad to see so many of you today. I see a few new faces, so before we start, I think I should explain a little about our group and why we meet. I founded this group seven years ago when my husband lost his life. I needed a place to talk to other people who've experienced the kind of loss I endured. With the encouragement of my siblings and my late husband's siblings, I created this space. With that in mind, would anyone like to start today?"

Everyone sits quietly, and a few people shuffle their feet and avert their gaze, as if she's going to pick someone at random.

"It doesn't have to be someone who's joining us for the first time today," she adds with a smile, encouraging us older members.

The sound of coughs and sniffles fill the room as we wait for someone to volunteer. I look around the room, noticing no one making a move to talk, and realization hits me like a brick wall.

It's going to have to be me.

Today is the day I share my story again.

"Hi, I'm Gwen." I stand up, making my way to the front of the room. Every time someone starts it reminds me of an AA meeting from TV. Everyone responds to an introduction the same way. "Hi, Gwen."

Once I'm at the front, I shift my weight between my feet. I count fifteen people, three of whom I don't recognize. "Most of you know my story, but like Gayle said, there are a few new faces today so why don't I share what brings me here?" I take in a deep breath as memories of that night two years ago flood my brain.

"Max is so excited," Dwayne says, leaning over to kiss me. "I can't back out now."

I shake my head and give a low laugh. "It's your funeral," I joke. "That kid just got his permit. I don't think it's absolutely necessary to take him out right this minute." I look over at our fifteen-year-old who is buckling himself in the driver's seat and checking the mirrors. But I know I'd have taken him if his dad didn't offer.

"If he drives like his mom then I trust I'm in good hands. After all, she drives like a grandma," Dwayne teases as he bends down for one final kiss before heading to the passenger side.

I stand at the top of the driveway, waving at my guys as Max slowly backs out.

Dwayne taking Max out for driving lessons should buy me a few hours of much needed time to myself, so once the car is out of view, I head back into the house and grab the book I've been slowly getting through.

I must've fallen asleep while reading, though, because all of a sudden, I'm being woken up to my phone ringing. I glance at the caller ID but don't recognize the number. "Hello?" I answer, apprehensively.

"Hello. This is Officer Decker with the Lancer County Sheriff's Office. Is this Mrs. Waters?" the voice on the other line asks.

As soon as the word "officer" is out of the man's mouth, my body goes on high alert. My eyes flash to the clock and I notice that four hours have passed since Dwayne and Max left. "This is her." My voice is almost a whisper. Maybe if I don't admit to being who he's looking for I won't hear the inevitable bad news.

"Ma'am, there's been an accident. Your son has obtained minor physical injuries but was unconscious when officers arrived on the scene. He's being transported to the hospital—"

I cut him off with a gut-wrenching sob. I'm breathing so heavily it takes a few seconds for me to register he's still speaking. "I'm sorry, can y—can you repeat that last part?"

"I'm sorry, ma'am. Your husband died on impact. His body is being transported to the medical examiner's office." I stop breathing. He couldn't have said what I think I heard. Dwayne couldn't have died. This is some sort of twisted prank he and Max concocted. It has to be.

The officer gives me the details regarding which hospital Max is being transported to, as well as the information for where I can go see Dwayne's body.

Fumbling with the keys sitting on the counter, I take a weak step toward the door.

This has to be a prank. I'm going to get down the road and Max and Dwayne will be standing outside the car with ice creams.

"It has to be a joke," I repeat to myself like a mantra.

I lock eyes with Paul as tears spill down my face. Gayle walks up to me with a box of tissues and wraps her warm arms around me. "Thank you for sharing. We're glad you're here with us," she says quietly to me. "Would anyone like to speak next?" She looks out at the crowd as I make my way back to my seat. When I sit down, I notice one of the newcomers is now standing up and introducing themselves.

Chapter 3

Paul

Hearing Gwen's story never gets easier, and she didn't even give the full account this time. I sit in the gray plastic chair, looking around the off-white walls that have posters of cute animals with inspirational quotes like, "Hang in There," and "Your Feelings are Valid," and "It's Okay to Not Be Okay."

I'm trying to concentrate as one of the new members, Cordelia, shares the unfortunate events that brought her here, but I'm failing miserably. My mind is in the past.

I step out of my truck, taking in a deep breath, trying to center myself. I've been coming here for three weeks and it still doesn't feel any easier. As I start to walk to the door, I notice a woman with short blonde hair, wearing a pair of white shorts and a light blue tank top. She's pacing back and forth, mumbling to herself at the entrance. After watching for a few moments, I decide to introduce myself.

"Hi. I'm Paul. Are you headed into the Lost Love Grief Group?" I reach my hand out toward her.

Her blue eyes widen as they slowly travel the length of my body and back up to my face. Pink fills the apples of her cheeks as she realizes that I caught her eyeing me.

"Yes. Hi, I'm Gwen. Are you headed in there too?" She places her cold hand in mine as we shake.

Nodding my head, I admit, "I am. I can walk in with you, if you'd like," and smile, watching her tuck a chunk of hair behind her ear.

"That would be great." She steps aside as I make my way to the door to open it. "Is this your first time here?" Gwen asks, as she walks into the lobby.

"Oh, no. This is my third."

"How recently did your spouse pass? If you don't mind me asking?" she asks, as she looks around the hall.

Taking in a deep breath, I close my eyes. "About four weeks ago. How about yours?" I open them back up and see sympathy etched on her features, a sad smile on her lips.

"My husband died five weeks ago. My son and I just moved here. When I told one of the women that works in the HR department about my recent loss she told me about this group. Her sister-in-law—Gayle, I think—is the founder."

My heart hurts for her and her son. I obviously knew she lost her spouse—that's why she's here—but I hate that it was relatively recent, and that a child lost their father to boot.

Gayle stands, thanks Cordelia for being brave enough to share, and extends her condolences before asking for more volunteers to speak. I share every week, but I have no intention of speaking today.

Today, I'm here to support others while I remember Sherri on my own. I don't want to burden the group with the reminder that it's the anniversary.

I must've zoned out—which is unlike me—because the next thing I know, everyone is standing up, preparing to leave, and Gwen is by my side.

"I'm going to grab Max and take him for a late lunch. Would you like to join us?" Her smile reaches her eyes as she awaits my answer.

I've met her seventeen-year-old a few times, but I got the impression he isn't thrilled his mom is friends with a man who isn't his dad. "I'm sorry, I can't today. I'm meeting with Tessa in about . . . forty minutes." I glance at my watch to make sure I'm not running late.

"Okay. Maybe next time. Tell her I say hello?" Gwen rests her hand on my bicep, and my eyes home in on the touch. I nod my head in agreement before she pulls back and heads for the door.

Quickly, I introduce myself to the three unfamiliar people who came to the meeting today before making my way to the truck. Tessa and I are meeting at Sherri's lake for a picnic. She planned on bringing Zigglers and told me to just bring myself.

As I drive, my mind wanders to Gwen.

She works as an engineer at a tech company in town. She's funny, beautiful, and smart. And her laugh makes me feel a lightness I haven't felt since I lost Sherri, but I can't ever tell her that.

I can't lie and say I don't find her attractive, but she's eight years younger than me. So even if I thought I could make good on Sherri's wish, I don't know if it could be with her.

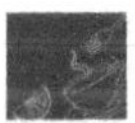

By the time I arrive at the lake, my mind has run through multiple reasons why I can never ask Gwen on a real date. The most important reason being, I'm simply not ready.

I don't know if my heart ever will be.

"Hi, Daddy." Tessa walks up to me with her arms outstretched and I pull her into a hug, holding the embrace a few seconds longer than normal.

"Hey, Bug. How're you feeling today?" I ask when I finally release her.

She walks back to her car, resting one hand on her growing baby bump as she reaches for the bags from Zigglers. "Besides this little lady kicking my ribs every twenty minutes, I'm doing okay . . . considering."

Grabbing the bags from her as she closes the door, I stop to admire how much she looks like her mother. Long, curly brown hair cascading down her back, bright brown eyes that make smoky quartz look dull, and her smile—so wide the corners of her eyes crinkle. It's such a blessing seeing that smile dance across her face again.

We walk down to the bench that sits on the dock and take a seat. The breeze makes the Virginia spring day slightly cooler than the norm for this time of year. Tessa reaches into the bag sitting next to her and pulls out two bottles of water. I reach into the other bag, grabbing the sandwiches tucked within. She hands me water as I hand her a sandwich.

"How was your appointment Friday?" I ask, knowing she and Graham got to see my granddaughter.

She swallows the bite she took before answering. "It went well. She's measuring a little big, but we both know what her dad looks like, so that's not surprising." She lets out a laugh, then asks, "How was your meeting?" before taking another bite of her grilled chicken sandwich.

I let my gaze flit around, observing the maple trees in bloom, the pine trees tall and proud, the flowers popping up through the grass and the soft ripples on the lake. "It was good. We had new members show up today, and Gwen shared parts of her story to start the meeting." My eyes find Tessa's, finding a familiar sadness there.

"Are you *ever* going to ask her out?" she asks, surprising me. "And I don't mean to those lunches y'all do after your meetings. I mean on a *real date*." Her eyes probe me questioningly.

I just shake my head. "It's not that simple, Tess." I sigh, fidgeting with the wrapper of my sandwich. "I'm not ready to start dating. Not yet."

Tessa takes a deep breath as she looks out at the water then back to me. "Dad . . . Mom wouldn't like this for you. You of all people should know that. She knew your heart—it's too big to stay lonely the rest of your life."

The rest of my life.

It's only been two years. That's a blink of an eye.

Looking at her, I briefly see my wife staring back at me and I blink as tears sting the back of my eyes. "I'm not alone. I have you, Graham, and soon I'll have Little Miss here." I force a laugh as I rub my hand over her belly.

She rolls her eyes as a scoff leaves her. "That's not what I mean, and you know it."

I nod my head as I look at the dock beneath my shoes. "I know what you mean, and I'll get there eventually. But right now, I just don't think I'm ready."

Chapter 4

Gwen

Max is lying on the couch watching a movie while I look through all the unpaid medical bills scattered across the table. I've had my job almost the whole time we've lived here, but insurance doesn't cover all of these expenses.

I'm shuffling the papers when I hear gasping—the tell-tale sign that it's about to happen again.

I drop everything and run to Max, kneeling down beside him and helping lower him to the floor—making sure he's lying on his side. I turn on the timer on my phone just as his eyes start to roll back and his body starts jerking, and I close my eyes for a moment as I take in a deep calming breath.

This isn't his first seizure and it won't be his last. Opening my eyes again, I run them over his body and around where he's lying, double-checking to make sure nothing is in his way. His arms are curled up against his chest, hands squeezed tight, head tilting back on its own accord, legs stretched out straight, and toes bending upward as his feet flex. As I'm taking another deep breath,

I'm met with the smell of urine. That's his least favorite part about all this—the loss of bladder control. When he wakes up he's going to be embarrassed, but it'll come out as anger.

I look down at my timer to make sure that it's still going. One minute and fifteen seconds. Max's body starts relaxing on the floor in front of me and I lean just a fraction closer. "Hey, baby, are you okay? What's your code word?" I ask, rubbing my hand through his sweaty golden locks.

His eyes blink a few times as his vision settles and he focuses on me. "Orange juice. And it's April eleventh. I'm fine, Mom. Now, let me go take a shower." As he pushes up from the ground I reach my arms out instinctively, in case the remnants of his seizure makes him lose his balance. Once he's fully up he pushes my arms out of the way and storms off to the bathroom.

I close my eyes as tears begin to build up. These damn seizures have taken my sweet boy and changed him. He used to be so happy and full of life. Now he goes to school and comes home only to lie on the couch or spend time in his room, alone. He used to be a typical teenage boy who wanted nothing to do with his parents and was embarrassed by me and Dwayne. Now, especially after his episodes, he goes through an angry and aggressive phase before reverting and acting as though he's my baby boy again—needing to feel the comfort of his mom. Thankfully they have lessened in frequency over the past year, but when he has one he becomes a completely different person for a few days.

I stand up to get the cleaning supplies so I can clean up the area where he had his accident. As I go through the motions, I think about what Paul said the last time we had lunch.

"If you need anything, just reach out. I'm only a phone call away."

I let my mind wander for a moment. What it would be like to call him and have him come over to help. He knows about Max—the whole sad story. He's never looked at me with pity though. Not like the men and women back in Lancer did. Those looks were the worst part, the last straw that pushed us out of that town.

Walking back to the table after I have the living room cleaned up, I stare at the papers in front of me. I take in a deep breath before exhaling, putting my elbow on the table and resting my cheek in my palm. I've learned a lot since losing Dwayne, but one of the most important things I wish we would have thought about before his untimely passing is finances. I wish we would have thought about taking out an insurance policy on him and myself in case of a situation like this, but we were either too naive to think something wouldn't happen to us, or too afraid to think of the possibility.

In the days that followed his death, I went and immediately took out an insurance policy on myself, leaving Max as the sole beneficiary in case something were to happen to me. Unfortunately, that's not something we had in place before Dwayne died. So, as I watch the invoices lying motionless on my table, I can't help but feel as if they're taunting me.

My eyes flick to my phone, and as much as I would love to reach for it and dial Paul's number, I can't. He said he'd help with anything, and at this current moment, *anything* is just a friendly ear to vent to. But I can't open myself up to that potential loss again. Losing Dwayne almost killed me. Truthfully, it probably would've done more damage than it did if Max didn't need me.

I pick up my phone, but instead of dialing Paul, I call the only other person I ever vent to.

My sister, Brandi.

Chapter 5

Paul

As I'm lying in bed, I stare at the wedding picture on my nightstand. Thirty-four years wasn't enough when we were supposed to have forever. Leaning over, I grab the envelope from its spot, taking out the letter for the fifth and final time today.

Watching the cancer ravage Sherri's body at such an alarming rate was the most difficult thing I've ever had to experience in my fifty-five years of life, and my heart pangs at the memories of her last few months. The diagnosis and treatment plan that gave us a glimmer of hope, then the inevitable news that the chemo was no longer working.

How am I supposed to open my heart to let someone else in when she still takes up every inch of it?

I clutch the letter to my chest before returning it to its safe space on the nightstand. Turning off the light, I roll over and face the empty side of the bed—her side—and let out a tired sigh. Sleeping alone in this bed hasn't gotten any easier over the last two years.

Morning comes too quickly, and I'm putting on my uniform, getting ready to head to the precinct when I notice the little flash on my cell phone alerting me to an unread text message.

Gwen:

> *It's been a rough day. It took me until late in the afternoon to realize what the date was. I hope you and Tessa were able to celebrate and grieve the way you needed to. Goodnight.*

I check the time of the message after reading the word "goodnight" and see that she sent it just after one in the morning. I can't help but wonder what was keeping her up.

Staring at my phone for a few moments, I have a silent debate with myself about whether or not I want to ask about the first part of her text. Can I be someone she confides in without opening my heart to her romantically?

Me:

> *Thanks. It was nice. We went to a spot Sherri enjoyed going to. Do you want to talk about what made your day so rough?*

I look at the text I typed out for a solid two minutes before deciding to hit send. Friends let friends unload their troubles on them, right?

I don't expect to hear back from her for a few more hours since it's four a.m. and her last text was sent so late, but a response comes through almost immediately.

Gwen:

Max had another seizure yesterday afternoon. His first one in two months. He was just finally starting to act more like his old self.

Gwen:

I feel so helpless. And on top of it, these medical bills seem to be duplicating themselves over night. It's never-ending.

Me:

Why are you awake so early? Is he okay? He was able to remember his code word and a current event, right? Do you need help looking over the bills? I'm no accountant, but I'm pretty decent at finding money where there doesn't seem to be any.

Me:

Damn, I just bombarded you with a million questions. I'm sorry.

Gwen:

Bold of you to assume I'm up early and not up late. He's okay, just his usual grumpy, tired self. He ate an early dinner and has been asleep since. As far as the help goes, I could never ask that of you.

Me:

Good thing you're not asking. I'm offering. When are they due?

I watch my phone, feeling desperate for her to respond—unsure what that means. I should really continue getting ready for work, but my heart is in my throat waiting to see if she's willing to accept my help. The thought of how much I care has me sitting down on the edge of the bed. I haven't felt a desire this strong to be there for someone outside of Tessa and Sherri. But knowing Gwen is struggling to the point where she's not sleeping because of the stress these bills are causing, makes my stomach ache with a feeling I can't put into words.

Gwen:

> *The first bunch are due by the thirtieth of this month. But I can't just accept this help for free. I will owe you dinner or something.*

Swallowing, I reread the last sentence four times. Is she saying that as friends or as a date? *Fuck.* I'm so out of practice I don't even know if this is still just a friend talking to a friend.

Chapter 6

Gwen

Did I really just accept Paul's help and then offer to take him to dinner? Will he think that's a date? Do I want it to be a date? I haven't gone on a date with someone that wasn't Dwayne in over twenty years.

I set my phone down and remind myself it can't be a date. I promised myself I wouldn't date again—not after losing my husband.

Just as I'm rolling over to try to finally get some sleep my door slowly opens and Max shuffles in. "Can I come lie with you?" his sleep-infused voice asks in a whisper.

"Of course, baby." I pull my covers back and scoot over to make room for him in the bed beside me. It's moments like these that break my heart, because I know this is his body's way of coming down after his seizure—the need to be comforted. My mind flashes to a seven-year-old Max climbing in bed with me and Dwayne. "You okay?"

He curls up in a ball with his back close to me. "I miss Dad." It comes out on a sigh.

I turn my body toward him and run my fingers through his hair, slightly scratching his head. "Me too, bud. Me too." We lie like this, with me rubbing his scalp until his body relaxes, breathing evens out, and light snores escape his mouth.

I look up at the clock on my dresser and see that it's six in the morning. I'm glad I took this week off to be home with Max while his school's on spring break, otherwise I'd have to climb out of bed, abandoning my sleeping son in what feels like a moment of need.

"How'd you sleep?" Max asks, as I walk in the kitchen, the earthy smell of coffee leading my way.

I grab my glass out of the cabinet and fill it up as I rub sleep out of my eyes. "Not nearly long enough. How about you?" I take that first sip of my black coffee, enjoying the bitterness as it hits my taste buds—thankful for coffee machines that can be set to start automatically.

He finishes his bowl of cereal before answering. "I woke up around five because I kept tossing and turning. I couldn't really fall back to sleep. That's why I decided to come to your room." He gives a small smile. "Your bed is always easier to fall asleep in on nights like that."

My heart tightens as emotions whirl through me. I'm glad that even at seventeen he still feels safe and comfortable enough to climb in bed with me if he needs to. "You're always welcome to come sleep with me when you need to, bud." I plant a kiss on his forehead as I make my way past him to sit at the table.

He stands and walks to the sink to clean his bowl before heading to the living room and plopping himself on the couch. My eyes follow him the whole time. The days following a seizure take a toll, making him pretty lethargic, and this being his first one in a few months, I'm expecting it to be a long day for him.

Once he's turned on the TV, my gaze bounces around the large room. Our house here in Middleburg is a lot smaller than what we had in Lancer, but that's when we had twice the income. When we first moved here we lived in a small, two-bedroom apartment on a month-to-month lease as I looked for a house. One day, I was driving around while Max was at school, and found a cute rent-to-own home just a short walk from the high school. We moved in two months after moving to town and have been here ever since. The living room doubles as our dining room, where there's a small table sitting near the entrance to the open-concept kitchen. A tan sectional couch takes up most of the living room, leaving enough space for a small coffee table in front.

Taking another sip of my coffee, I look down at the bills still strewn across the table. I let out a sigh in defeat as I pull my laptop close so I can look at my budget for the month. "Payday is on the fifteenth, which is Thursday . . ." I mumble to myself as I try to decide what needs to be paid first.

I must have gotten lost in the work because the next thing I know, Max is setting a plate down on top of the paper I was looking at. "You need to eat something. It's two, and all you've had since you woke up is"—he eyes my mostly-full cup—"maybe three sips of coffee."

My eyes feel misty as a flashback of Dwayne and I when we first got together comes rushing to the forefront of my mind.

"Babe, you need to eat. You've been staring at that textbook for hours," Dwayne says as he waves a burger in front of my face.

I blink a few times as my eyes adjust to the room around me. The smell of greasy burgers and salty fries assault my senses as I take in the fast food bag sitting in between Dwayne and myself.

"When did you get food?" I ask him in shock. We just started studying. When did he leave?

"I left about twenty minutes ago to get it. Like I said, you've been staring at that book for hours. It's time you ate something." A husky chuckle leaves his chest.

I set aside my study materials as I reach for the burger he's holding out to me. "Sorry. I just got so focused on my work, I didn't even register that you left."

"It's not a big deal. But you need to take a break every now and then to make sure you eat something. That beautiful brain of yours needs sustenance if it's going to keep getting bigger."

Rolling my eyes I steal a fry. "Did you at least finish studying for your final before you left to get food?"

He shakes his head as he takes a sip of his drink. "I finished studying for that final and started working on my next study guide before leaving."

"Damn, I really was in the zone. You got all that done?"

Dwayne laughs again, dimples on display as his whole face lights up. "Just eat your food, nerd."

"Hey!" I yell, throwing a French fry at his face.

I look up at Max, who has his father's caring heart, tall, naturally muscular frame, and dimples that have always made me envious. He has my golden-blond hair, blue eyes, and the ability to take everything to heart.

"Your dad used to do that." I pick up one of the chips from my plate.

He quirks an eyebrow in question. "What?"

I let out a soft chuckle and motion to the sandwich and chips. "Get me food when I was lost in whatever work I was caught up in."

Max pulls a chair closer to me before sitting down. "I remember. He once told me that when you're caught up in a project, it's our duty to make sure you don't forget to take care of yourself."

"That definitely sounds like something he would say," I say with a smile. "So, is there anything you're in the mood to do today?" I ask, taking a bite of the turkey and cheese sandwich he made.

Chapter 7

Paul

On my way home from work, I stop at Leroy's and pick up the usual for Tessa, Graham, and myself. Stuffed mushroom pasta and meatballs with extra garlic knots for Tessa, zesty barbeque ribs and fries for Graham, and fried chicken enchiladas with queso and green chili sauce for me. The best thing about Leroy's is that the smorgasbord of food works, even though it probably shouldn't.

Getting back in the truck, I shoot off a text in the group chat letting them know I'm on my way. One of my favorite aspects of having my daughter marry the boy down the street—I get to see them for dinner just about every night. Tonight, it's my choice for dinner and Tessa's choice for entertainment, which always has me on my toes.

Me:

Picked up dinner. On my way.

Graham:

Perfect! Tessa's starting to get hangry, and you know how much worse it's gotten since she's been pregnant.

Tessa:

Do you want to sleep on the couch tonight?

Graham:

Shutting up now.

Tessa:

Probably a good idea.

Me:

Maybe I'll drop dinner off and hide out at my house for the night.

Tessa:

Perfect. Take Graham with you.

I roll my eyes as the conversation between the two of them continues in the chat, causing my phone to light up. Buckling my seatbelt, I turn the phone over so I don't get distracted and head toward home.

Before I turn the ignition off, Tessa has the passenger side door open and is reaching for the bag of food. I watch in astonishment as she pulls her garlic knots out and inhales two of them before she even acknowledges me.

"Hey, Daddy," she says, her mouth still full.

Chuckling, I shake my head at the sight before me. "Hey, Bug. Hungry?" That must be the wrong thing to say because she jerks her head up, gives me a death glare, grabs the food bags, and stomps back into her house.

Two hours later, Tessa is snuggled up close to Graham as we play Clue. Why I'm allowing her to be so close to him when this is a very secretive game, I'm not sure. Maybe because she finally returned to her joyful self after getting food in her and I don't want to risk poking the bear.

"I think it was . . ." She looks down at her clue sheet before shifting her eyes between me and Graham. "Professor Plum, with the lead pipe, in the . . ." She glances down at which room her character is in before finishing. "Living room." Again, her gaze bounces between her husband and I.

"I can prove you wrong," Graham says cautiously, earning a scowl from Tessa. She whips her head at me and I hold my hands up and shake my head.

She huffs and narrows her eyes. "Ugh. Show me." When Graham shows her his card she squeals, shimmies, and makes a mark on her paper. "Your turn, Daddy." She smiles brightly at me.

I take my turn, making a guess—which Tessa smugly proves wrong—then Graham takes a turn, unable to make a guess, before it's Tess's turn again. This time she grabs the envelope in the middle of the board and says, matter-of-factly, "I know the answer. It was Miss Scarlett, with the lead pipe, in the lounge."

I scrunch my nose at her declaration because only one of those is something she guessed the last round. She shakes her shoulders as she goes to reveal the answer, and I drop my jaw as she sets down the corresponding cards that match her guess.

"How? You only guessed like two rooms the whole game," I ask as I look at the clues marked on my paper.

She gives a soft chuckle before turning her cards over—five out of six are locations on the board. The other, Professor Plum. I shake my head in disbelief and Graham just beams at his wife as she participates in a celebratory dance for one. The spitting image of her mom when she would win a game.

"Your turn, Mom," Tessa says, as she stares at the board, assessing.

Sherri spins the spinner and taps her fingers on her knees, waiting for it to stop. Tessa's roommate, Nell, watches as it slows. "Damn," Nell whispers when she realizes that Sherri can change salary cards with any player.

Tapping her chin, she looks at the group sitting around The Game of Life board on the coffee table. "I think I want to take Nellie's one-hundred thousand dollar salary. Too bad I can't get that salary in real life." She hands her measly twenty-thousand dollar salary card to Nell as she grabs her new one.

Tessa covers her laugh with her hand as Nell's face scrunches up. "Remind me why I always let you Gunters talk me into playing a game every time Mama and Papa Gunter come visit?" Nell asks, taking a sip from her glass of wine.

The game continues with Sherri well in the lead. Somehow, she keeps getting the high numbers when spinning, while the rest of us get ones, twos, and threes. Before long, Sherri is nine spaces away from the retirement space, and it's her turn to go again.

We all watch with bated breath as the spinner slows. Ten. Of course. Sherri lets out a squeal and bounces in her spot on the floor, looking up at us and wiggling her eyebrows.

"So, when are you going to ask Gwen out on a date?" Tessa asks, not for the first time, while cleaning up the mess from dinner.

I blink at her as Graham mumbles, "Babe!" But it doesn't surprise me that she's asking. She knows the relationship that we've built and knows what her mom wanted for me.

"We're going to have dinner later this month," I answer. Technically not lying.

She stops what she's doing and stares at me. "Did you just say you're having dinner with her? As in the meal *after* lunch? As in the meal at the end of the day?" She holds my gaze, daring me to back down.

"Yep. We haven't set a specific day yet, but we discussed it this morning." My response must be acceptable to her because she stops staring and continues on with her task.

As I give them goodbye hugs before I walk outside, Tessa whispers in my ear, "Mom would be happy you're taking a risk with your heart."

I give a small smile as I head out. If only she knew I didn't plan on taking any risks at all.

Chapter 8

Gwen

Tuesday morning I find myself lying on my stomach in front of the TV, holding a controller, playing old school video games with Max. A few months back he found a seller online who had a vintage SEGA with some games in good condition and bought it.

"Oh, you are so going down, Mama!" Max yells as he presses on his controller aggressively.

I laugh before hitting the arrow buttons, taking my character out of direct contact with his. He wanted to play *Mortal Kombat*, but he underestimated how good I'd be, considering I grew up playing this game. I steal a glance at him as he relaxes his body, thinking I've given up, allowing me to make my move.

"What the fuck? Where did that move come from?" Max groans as I come out the victor. He studies me before tossing his controller to the side. "Do you want to order pizza for lunch?" he asks as he moves to a seated position and fiddles with the hem of his shorts.

"Yeah, pizza sounds good. Go ahead and grab my phone and order what you want. I'll be right back," I say, standing up to head to the bathroom.

Afterward, I head back to the living room, expecting to see Max ready to play another round, but instead, I see him staring at my phone. "Get the pizza ordered?" I ask, plopping myself next to him. He flinches at the movement. "Everything okay, bud?"

He looks up at me with hurt in his eyes. Holding out my phone, I notice he has my text thread with Paul open. "He wanted to know when you wanted him to come over, or if it would be best to meet at his place."

I grab my phone and set it aside without looking to see what the new text says. "He's just going to help me with something." My voice is tinged with guilt. I don't even know if I believe myself.

"And that's why you were talking about me and my *episode* the other night?" he asks while standing up. "I'm sorry my seizures are so *rough* on you. You know what, forget pizza. I'm not hungry."

Before I have a chance to respond to him, he's taking off down the hall to his room. I stand up to follow behind him but am met with the sound of his door slamming. Closing my eyes I take a deep breath, hold for five, release for five. I repeat this three times before picking up my phone.

Paul:

> *So, we never discussed what day would be best for me to come over? Or would you prefer coming over here? I'm pretty flexible, so whatever works best for you.*

Paul:

> *How's Max feeling today?*

This new message doesn't mention it being a rough day, so he must have scrolled a little. I should be angry with him for reading my texts, but instead, I'm angry with myself. I shouldn't be confiding in another man.

I look up at a family picture hanging on the wall. We were so happy. Dwayne would have helped me look through these bills and our finances to see if there's something I missed. I wouldn't have even had to consider asking Paul.

No. If Dwayne were still here, there wouldn't be any medical bills, I would still be in Lancer because there wouldn't have been an accident, and therefore, I never would've even met Paul.

Taking another deep breath, I sit back on the couch, keeping my gaze on the family photo. "Fuck. I miss you so much, Dwayne. I don't know what to do. I feel like every decision I make is wrong, and every complicated feeling I have is disrespectful toward you." Shaking my head, a single tear slips down my cheek.

Max clearly isn't comfortable with my friendship with Paul, not that I fully blame him. But he doesn't dictate who I get to be friends with, because that's what Paul is—a friend. I *need* friends. It's fucking lonely here. Paul helping me just has to stay that way—strictly friends. I can't allow for it to become more.

Chapter 9

Paul

Gwen decided on me coming to her place on Friday, making me uncharacteristically nervous through-out the week. *I'm going over to help her with her bills. What about that is worth being anxious over?*

The week went by excruciatingly slow, too, adding to my building anxiety.

I'm thankful to be on the night shift tonight because I'm able to go to her house this morning. She felt like Max would be less spooked about another guy coming to the house during the day, while he's home.

Sitting in my truck outside of her home, I take a minute to collect myself. I look at the modest white house. A blue door sits at the center of the small front porch, which is home to one single rocking chair. The lawn appears to be freshly cut with beautiful zinnias lining the walkway leading up to the door and a single dogwood tree in the middle of the lawn. I take in a deep breath before picking up the cobbler I made. If I've learned anything from my son-in-law, it's never show up to someone's house emp-ty-handed.

"This is not a date," I mutter to myself as I make my way to the door. "It isn't a date."

I knock twice before a tall, blond-haired, blue-eyed boy opens the door. He stands in the doorway, assessing me, arms crossed, eyes narrow as they roam over my body, out to my truck in the driveway, then back to me.

"My mom's in the dining room," he says before stepping aside.

I smile, giving a small nod. "Thanks. I brought some peach cobbler if you want any," I offer as I hold up the dish. Max's sharp gaze shifts from my face to my outstretched hand and, without saying anything, he turns, effectively dismissing me.

I quickly toe off my shoes before shutting the door behind me. When I turn back around, Gwen is standing a few feet away with a nervous smile on her face.

"Thanks for coming over this morning. We can go back to the table. What is that?" she says in quick succession, pointing at the Tupperware I'm holding.

I smile wide and hold it up. "I made cobbler."

Taking it from me, she opens the lid and sniffs, the smell of peaches and vanilla filling the small space. I made it this morning, so its scent is still strong.

We walk a few feet into what is set up as the dining area, but could also still be considered part of the living room. As Gwen heads into the kitchen to set down the dessert I take the time to look around. I notice pictures hanging on the walls—a lot like my house. Mostly of Max through the years, but every few frames there's a family photo, or one of Gwen and who I'm assuming is her late husband, Dwayne.

My eyes are locked on a picture hanging next to the table, of the two of them cutting the cake at their wedding, when Gwen comes up next to me. "I told him if he shoved that cake in my face he would *not* be having a fun wedding night." She chuckles at the memory, and I notice the glint in his eyes is mischievous, like he was contemplating if putting the cake in her face was worth the threat she promised.

"So, did he?" I turn to face her, momentarily shocked by how gorgeous she is, even though she's clearly lacking sleep. Her long nose has a slight bump in the middle, her shoulder-length blonde hair is disheveled, and dark circles form under her eyes—evidence that her face is clean of makeup. She's wearing a red, oversized T-shirt with *LHS JV Football* across the front and a pair of black biker shorts. I'm not sure why, but the knowledge that she didn't feel the need to get dressed up for me is oddly comforting—reassuring that this is in fact, not a date.

Before answering she takes a seat at the table, a stack of paper and a laptop in front of her. "He did not. But he never told *me* not to, so I pushed a piece in his." She scrunches her nose and I can't help but smile at her admission, imagining the couple from the picture laughing as a younger Gwen shoves a slice of wedding cake into her new husband's face.

Gwen rests her forehead in her hands as she looks down at the stack of papers sitting in front of her. "This is so embarrassing," she says slightly under her breath, but I catch it nonetheless. We've been working on this budget for two hours and it's almost time for me to leave so I can get ready for work.

"What is?" I lean my face down, trying to look her in the eyes.

"Needing help with finances. I'm a forty-seven-year-old woman, I *should* be better at this. Or better yet, I should've hired an accountant so these bills wouldn't have gotten so out of control." Her blue eyes look as though she's fighting back tears.

I reach my hand over and rest it on the one she just laid on the table. "Gwen, there's nothing to feel embarrassed about. Money is hard to deal with. Everyone needs help every now and then, and I think it takes someone strong to admit it and actually ask for it. I commend you for taking me up on my offer to come take a look."

A small huff leaves her, and a smile creeps across her face as she picks up some paper. "So, I can have these bills paid off with this money here?" she asks, holding up three invoices and pointing to an amount on her computer.

I shake my head as I finger through a few papers I have in my hand. "You could also pay this one off too. But looking at your average spending from the past two months, you might have to skip a take-out meal . . . or three."

Max walks up holding a bottle of water and a plate with a sandwich on it. "Here, Mom. You haven't eaten anything all day." He places the items on the table and stares me down. "Dad would want me to make sure you're fed and taken care of."

I assume he's trying to make a point, that he can take care of his mom, which makes me smile. Even though I never met his dad, I know he'd be proud.

"Thanks, Hon," Gwen says as she smiles up at her son. "We're just about done here and I was going to ask if you wanted a bite of that cobbler Paul made. I don't think he knew peaches were your favorite."

Max's cheeks turn a faint shade of red. "I don't want any cobbler. I've decided to give up unnecessary sugars to see if that helps my seizures.

She sticks out her bottom lip a fraction before she nods her head once and shrugs. "Okay then. More for me." Her eyebrows raise as she turns her focus back on me. "Which one was it that I'll be able to pay if I cut back on the *fast food and unnecessary sugars?*"

Chapter 10

Gwen

"Thank you again for helping me make a plan of attack to get these medical bills paid off. And for the cobbler," I say, as Paul and I make our way to his truck. Honestly, words don't feel like enough of a thanks because he helped me look at my finances *and* make a goal so I can have the rest paid by the end of the month.

The laugh lines on his face deepen as a smile spreads across it. "It was my pleasure. If you need any more help you know how to reach me." He opens his door and begins to climb in, the fabric of his jeans hugging his ass as he lifts one leg up to get into the cab, causing heat to form in my core at the sight.

I blink a few times to stop myself from checking him out before he catches me. "So, about that dinner?" I rush out as he moves to shut the door.

"When would you like to do that?" His voice is deep as he questions me.

Taking a swallow as inconspicuously as possible, I respond, "Max is staying with a friend tomorrow night—" I look over my shoulder at the house then turn back to

Paul. "That is . . . if you don't already have plans." My palms feel sweaty but I don't want to rub them on my shorts and risk making it obvious that there's a sudden rush of nerves that just jolted through my body.

He pulls out his cell phone and taps on it a few times. "Tomorrow night works. What time should I pick you up?" The way he asks has me second-guessing if he understands this is platonic. I *need* it to be platonic.

"I can just meet you there. Wherever *there* is," I say, chewing on my bottom lip.

A flash of what looks like relief flits in his eyes. "Okay. Any particular place you'd like to go?" he asks, rolling his window down before he shuts the door.

"We could do Zigglers? I could go for a good hoagie."

He agrees, telling me to text him if there's any change in plans before we say our goodbyes and he puts his truck in reverse, backing out of the driveway.

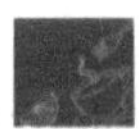

This is *not* a date. So why does my stomach feel like there are a million butterflies fighting for attention in my stomach right now? I've tried on six different outfits and am currently standing in front of the mirror in my seventh. The April weather is being finicky tonight, making it feel like winter again with a temperature in the forties.

I twist my hips around so I can get a look at my backside as best as I can. I'm wearing a pair of light denim jeans that are high enough in the waist to tuck in the mom pooch I never lost after having Max, a blush pink sweater that shows off a modest amount of cleavage, and a pair of black ankle boots. I check the time on my phone and realize this outfit has to be the one because I have exactly twenty-three minutes to drive across town so I'm not late.

I walk into Zigglers with one minute to spare and immediately spot Paul resting his arms on a high-top table. Taking a moment before he notices me, I check out my *not* date. He's wearing a pair of dark denim jeans that hug his thighs, a pair of black shoes, and a light gray Henley that molds against his unfairly muscled arms. The traitorous insects in my belly start to go crazy again as I realize how attracted to this man I am.

As I start to walk over to him, he glances my way and our eyes lock, his piercing blue eyes stopping me in my tracks. Once my brain finally sends the signal to my legs to start working he stands up to wait for me to make it to the table.

"You look nice," he compliments me as he goes to pull out the chair I stopped behind.

Briefly forgetting what I'm wearing, I look down. "Thanks. So do you."

After I've taken my seat, he walks back to his. "Do you already know what you want?" he asks, holding a menu in my direction.

Shaking my head yes, I take the menu anyway to give me something to do with my hands. "I really do appreciate you coming by yesterday and helping. I didn't think I was that bad with money, but I just couldn't figure out how to make it work with what I had in my budget." I start to ramble, repeating the same thing I told him yesterday.

The waitress comes to take our order—a lemonade and a meatball hoagie for me, a sweet tea and an Italian hoagie for Paul—then I look around the small restaurant. This is where Paul and I come when we grab lunch after our meetings so I've become very familiar with its atmosphere. There are tall tables like the one we're at, as well as small circular tables placed strategically around the dining area. At the back of the restaurant there's a small counter where you can place to-go orders with a sign hanging on the wall with the specials for the day. He brought a group of us here after my first time going to LLGG. Sometime between that first trip and now it's become a habit.

"I'm sorry if I made Max uncomfortable with my being there," Paul says, getting my attention.

I wave my hand as if to shake his apology off. "Don't apologize. He's a moody teenager who isn't used to sharing his mom with other people anymore." The waitress brings our drinks and I immediately take a sip of mine. "I haven't really made it a priority to make friends and create relationships outside of those I talk to at group and my coworkers who I, admittedly, only talk to out of necessity," I say.

Paul watches me intently as he fiddles with the paper from the straw wrapper, letting me share without interruption. "I know it's important to have friends, and do things for myself, but I have this fear . . . that if I'm not home or close by if Max needs me then I'll lose him too. Him being at his friend's house tonight is actually really difficult for me. He hasn't stayed with anyone since his seizures began. Kyle has stayed with us and we've explained, ad nauseam, to him and his mom what to do should he have a seizure in front of them, but I just worry."

I widen my eyes, rolling them to look at the corner of the ceiling, fighting back tears that are forming. I've never shared this with anyone, and I'm not sure why I'm sharing it now, besides the fact that Paul makes me feel comfortable. "I can't lose him too." The last part comes out as a whisper.

Paul hesitates as he reaches his hand across the table to mine. I flip my palm up, accepting this form of comfort. "I can't imagine that fear you have. You lost Dwayne so suddenly, and to live with the constant fear that you might lose your child just as quickly . . . that's unimaginable."

I close my eyes as a tear escapes. "I'm sorry. You hear enough sad stories during group and I'm sure at work. Let's talk about something else—*anything* else." Encouraging Paul to change the subject, I pick up the fork in front of me and play with it.

He puckers his lips in thought and my mind immediately wonders what it would be like to be kissed—tasted—by them. He's probably a tender lover with how caring he is. Shaking my head, I try to focus on anything but his mouth. My gaze travels to his hand still holding mine, he's rubbing his thumb back and forth on my wrist, the touch sending a shiver up my arm.

Before he gets a chance to say anything, I blurt, "What is this? I'm too old to play games. Is this . . ." I gesture between the two of us. "Are we here just as me repaying you for helping me out, or . . . is this a date?" Sucking in a deep breath, I chew on the inside of my lip as I wait for his response.

Sitting up straighter, he pulls his hand from mine, making me feel an odd sensation of loneliness. He huffs out a breath, causing his cheeks to puff out. "Well . . ." He looks at his hands now sitting under the table on his lap. "Would you like it to be a date?" He looks up slightly through his eyelashes. The move makes him look twenty years younger and I can easily see why Sherri loved him so much.

I continue gnawing on my lip as I contemplate the question he threw at me. Do I want this to be a date? Yes. I'm very clearly attracted to him and would love to see if he feels the same. But also, no. I have no intention of ever dating to fall in love again, and I don't think I could date Paul *without* falling.

I just can't put myself in the position to lose another person I love.

Chapter 11

Paul

Forcing myself to blink so I don't look insane, I realize I'm sitting so still I think I forget to breathe as I wait for Gwen to answer. I don't know what I want her to say. On one hand, yes, I would love for this to be a date. Tessa is right, Sherri wouldn't want me to put off dating forever. Plus, she looks gorgeous. Not that I've ever seen her *not* looking gorgeous. But on the other hand, am I really ready to be on a date with someone that isn't Sherri?

My eye catches on the waitress as she sets our subs down on the table. I thank her before she walks away, then turn my attention back to Gwen. She blows a soft raspberry with her mouth, causing my gaze to get stuck on her plump lips. I can't help as the thought of what those lips might taste like enters my mind. Lemonade, perhaps?

What the hell? Why don't I admit I'd like this to be a date?

Right as I go to speak, she says, "Why don't we consider this my repayment?"

I feel my chest deflate, and I hope the disappointment can't be read on my face.

I nod my head once before picking up my sub and taking a bite. Looking around the restaurant, I try to think of anything else to say to take the tension out of the air. I take a peek at her and see her picking at her dinner.

"Want to talk about what's on your mind?" I put my food down, giving her my full attention.

"It's just—" She sucks in a big breath. "I said I'm too old for games, so I should be honest." My back goes rigid as I wait to see where she's going with this. "Your friendship over the past two years has been a breath of fresh air. The friends I have from back home *still* walk on eggshells when we talk, afraid of saying the wrong thing. But you . . . you talk to me without pussyfooting around topics, which is so . . . liberating." She takes a sip of her drink as she looks around the dining space. "I think having you be so open about your past and allowing me to be open about mine has led me to develop feelings that might possibly be more than friendship, and quite honestly, that scares the shit out of me." Her blue eyes shine as she searches my face for some kind of reaction.

Honesty. It's refreshing hearing someone be so candid. *Okay, I can do this too.* I quickly inhale. "Gwen, I just want to thank you for telling your truth—for sharing something that seems a bit scary. It's not often someone is willing to open up and be raw like that . . . Now, it's my turn to be frank, because I agree, we're too old for games. Let's leave those for someone Max's age." She gives a small chuckle and I take another calming breath.

Honesty. I can do this. "Sherri wrote me a letter before she passed telling me to find someone that can make me happy again—someone I could share the little moments with. I reread that letter multiple times a day, trying to understand how that could be possible." A lump forms in my throat thinking about Sherri's letter—sharing the personal things she wrote to me. "When I met you, I thought that we would talk when we saw each other during group, maybe grab lunch or drinks occasionally with some other people after. What I didn't anticipate was our friendship turning into what it's become. If I'm being truthful, I believe my feelings for you might also be a little stronger than friendship, or at least, could easily grow into more."

When I take another pause to collect my thoughts, we're interrupted by Gwen's cell phone ringing. She picks it up to look at the caller ID and her eyes go wide. "I have to get this."

I nod, acknowledging that she should take it.

I try my best not to eavesdrop but the panic in her tone puts me on high alert.

"What happened?" she asks the person on the other line. "Did he fall? Was he on the floor already? Is he awake? How long?" All of these questions come flying out of her mouth quicker than I imagine the caller can answer.

"I'll be right there," I hear her say before she hangs up. Turning her attention to me, she starts collecting her things. "I'm so sorry, Paul. Max had a seizure at his friend's house and when he came to he was in a bit of a panic and was asking for me. I have to go."

"Don't apologize, go—go! I'll take care of the check. I'll get this packed up and I can drop it off at your house on my way home. Would Max want anything to eat?" I ask, waving the waitress down to ask for the check and to-go boxes.

"He might want a club, but only if you don't mind. I really am sorry, but I have to go." She stands up and starts running out the door.

I order a club to go, pay the check, pack up our leftovers, and leave a fifty percent tip.

Stopping by her house on my way home, I notice her car isn't in the driveway. She must not have made it back from picking Max up. I write a quick note and stick it in the bag of subs before walking up to the porch and leaving them by the door.

I'm not sure where we stand after our confessions, but I feel lighter after having told her how I feel.

Chapter 12

Gwen

It takes twenty minutes to get to Kyle's from Zigglers, and that's with driving a questionable speed for someone who has a fear of getting in a car accident. Unbuckling my seatbelt before I'm fully parked, I open the door and run to the porch where Max and Esther are sitting.

"Thank you so much for calling me," I say to Esther as I pull Max in for a hug. Both panic and embarrassment swirl in his features. "Where's Kyle?"

Esther looks at Max who shifts uncomfortably in my hug. "He told me goodbye before I came outside." He pulls out of my grasp and bends down to grab his stuff. "I'm going to wait in the car. Don't take too long talking." I roll my eyes at his comment, but he's not wrong; I do tend to talk longer than necessary.

"Kyle got scared seeing Max have his seizure. I know you and Max have both discussed what happens when he has one, but I think he wasn't as prepared as he thought he would be." Kyle's mom explains why he isn't out here. "He started crying and felt really bad that he couldn't do anything but watch."

I nod my head in understanding. "It's really terrifying to witness, especially that first time you see it happen. No amount of reading up on it, or being told what to expect, can truly prepare you for it." I don't want Kyle to feel guilty for not feeling brave at that moment. "I'm sure if Max is upset now he'll calm down and think about it from Kyle's perspective. Everything will be okay." Hopefully, I'm not lying.

When I get in the car, Max has his seat leaned back and his eyes closed but I'm not sure if he fell asleep or is just resting. Turning the car on, I immediately shut off the radio in case he did fall asleep. He always needs rest after a seizure—it zaps the energy right out of him.

"I think I lost my only friend," Max mumbles from the seat beside me.

I take a quick glance at him as I pull up to a stop sign. "What makes you say that, bud?" I hold my breath, waiting for the part where he shuts down and brushes off my question.

He surprises me by sitting his seat up, looking out the window as he responds. "We were playing video games and I made that awful gasping noise that happens before I have one. Luckily, I was already on the floor so I didn't have to move myself." He sits quietly for a minute before he continues. "I didn't put the remote down before my arms jerked and I yanked his console from the entertainment center. I obviously didn't find that out until after, but Kyle was pretty upset—he was crying. Not only do I think I broke his game, but I'm also the kid who pisses themselves and shakes like a fish out of water. He's not gonna want to be friends with me anymore."

My heart breaks for Max as he shares what happened and the reason he thinks Kyle was crying—what might be the true reason he was crying. I risk another look at my son as he continues to stare out the window, his reflection giving away a tear that's sliding down his cheek.

"Baby, I've met Kyle before. He doesn't seem like the kind of kid who would hold any of that against you. And we told him what to expect if you were to ever have one in front of him. I know it was scary for him, but he knew you would more than likely lose control of your bladder. If anything, I think he was scared. You and I have talked about fight-or-flight reflexes. Crying could be his body's way of handling that fear." Pulling into our driveway, I finish my speech. "I wouldn't count him off yet. Seeing a seizure for the first time is a lot for anyone."

He looks at me and shrugs his shoulders. "I guess," is all he says before getting out of the car and heading toward the house.

Reaching into the back seat, I grab his bag and my purse, then I make my way to the door. Before I get there, I see a plastic bag on the doorstep and a smile cracks across my face. Paul actually brought the leftovers.

"Food!" Max says as soon as he notices the bag on the step. He bends down and picks it up, passing me a note without reading it but keeping the boxes for himself.

I make my way in front of him to unlock the door and push it open. He walks to the table, sitting down and rifling through the bag as I take my time setting stuff by the door so I can read the note.

Gwen,

I'm sorry you had to leave without finishing your dinner. I really hope everything is okay with Max. I enjoyed being able to talk to you and open up a bit more. I hope we can get together soon to finish our conversation.

Paul

The butterflies from before dinner return with a vengeance as I'm reminded of what I admitted during our *not* date. I like him more than a friend, but I wasn't lying when I told him it scares me. I wasn't planning on ever liking someone again. I had already come to terms with it just being Max and I until he grows up and meets someone to start a family with.

Then I met Paul, and really got to know him. Over the past two years, my heart has been slowly opening itself up to the possibility of allowing a place for him inside. His kindness toward not only me and the others at LLGG, but when he's been around Max and when I've seen him with Tessa and her husband, has my heart telling me he's someone worth letting in. But my mind keeps telling me I'm not ready.

"Are you sure you don't want to come with us?" Paul asks the group gathered by the door before we leave our meeting.

"I can't. I have to go meet up with my son," Gayle says.

Rodney shakes his head. "Sorry, I can't today. Maybe next week?"

The others just shake their heads and give a wave over their shoulders as they walk outside.

"I'm still in," I say, pushing my purse up higher on my shoulder. The group that grabs coffee after LLGG has slowly dwindled the past few weeks, but I've enjoyed the adult interaction outside of work for the past year and a half.

The smile that spreads across his face is achingly handsome, causing my breath to catch. He lifts his arm up, gesturing for me to head out ahead of him.

When we get to the parking lot, I look around and see that it's already emptied out. Everyone wasn't joking when they said they had to get out of here. "Do you want to meet me there or do you want to ride over together?"

"I think I should meet you there, in case I need to leave to get to Max."

Paul nods his head. "Sounds good."

About ten minutes later, I'm sitting at a table in Arlynes with a mug of hazelnut coffee in my hand. "Max played football on the JV team back in Lancer, and he was on the football team in middle school. His doctor never said he wouldn't be able to play now, with his seizures, but he's shown no interest in trying out for the team." I take a sip of my drink and tilt my eyes toward him.

"I can see why he'd be nervous about it. I'm not sure if the doctors have pinpointed his triggers, and it could be scary to think about, being out on the field and unexpectedly having one." Paul's eyes bore into mine as he speaks.

Nodding, I set my mug down. "I know, and if I'm being honest . . . the thought of him putting on a helmet and getting back on the field terrifies me. His seizures are so sporadic we never know when one is going to happen. We don't know what his exact triggers are, we just know they happen out of the blue."

I bite my lip as I think about Max's last seizure. We had been sitting down to eat dinner, and he said he was feeling weird. He went to stand up, but as soon as he stood he started gasping. I was out of my seat and guiding him to the floor so fast I could have put the Flash out of work. When we spoke to his neurologist about it, he said it sounds like Max is developing auras, which is nice—if he has them all the time.

"Well, if he ever wants to toss the football around or anything, I played back in the day, and Graham is one of the football coaches at the middle school. It can just be tossing the ball back and forth. Maybe that'll help him feel a little normal again."

The fact that Paul is offering solutions to help Max feel like his old self again has my heart hurting in an unexpected way.

I look over at Max, realizing that Paul did in fact get him a hoagie too, and I can't help but watch as he sits there, stuffing his face, while I'm over here with a war being waged inside my body.

Chapter 13

Paul

Wednesday comes faster than expected. I roll out of bed and obsessively check my phone. I haven't heard from Gwen since she texted a brief message Saturday evening, thanking me for dinner and informing me she wasn't going to make it to group on Sunday morning because she wanted to make sure Max didn't have any more seizures.

I release a frustrated sigh as I see no new notifications, then I check to make sure my volume is turned all the way up before tossing my phone on the bed. As I'm putting on my uniform, I glance at my nightstand. It takes me a moment to register that I haven't opened Sherri's letter in a few days. My heart aches at that realization.

Pulling it out of its safe place, I open it and run my fingers over the edge of the paper. My eyes roam over the familiar words, catching on one line in particular.

Don't close yourself off from loving again.

Not that I think my feelings for Gwen resemble love, but I do find it hard to stay away. I want to talk to her, hear about her day, listen to her talk about Max and how he's doing. Smiling slightly, I can't help but think . . . maybe I won't let Sherri down after all.

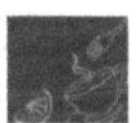

I'm sitting at my desk looking at paperwork from a few arrests that were made this morning when there's a knock on my door. "Come in!" I say loud enough to be heard through the wood.

"Hey, Daddy," Tessa greets, pushing the door closed behind her. "I know we're supposed to have dinner tonight, but we have to cancel, so I thought I'd stop by for lunch." She holds up a bag that smells suspiciously like greasy burgers.

I stand up to clear a space at my desk while motioning for her to take a seat. "You have to cancel? Why?" I ask as I create neat piles of paper for later me to sift through.

As she pulls out two burgers wrapped in foil she replies, "Graham's parents *finally* reached out to him, and we're going to have dinner with them. Grant and his family will be there too—to act as a buffer—in case things get uncomfortable."

Graham hasn't had a relationship with his parents in over a decade, so this is a shock. My hands stop moving and I go still. "How does he feel about this?" I stand to my full height and face her.

"Would you sit down? I'm not some criminal you need to intimidate with that stance." She chuckles as she tosses a fry at me. "He's nervous. The last time he spoke with them they told him they weren't exactly thrilled with his life choices," Tessa says, taking a bite of her cheeseburger.

I nod my head, thinking of the story Graham shared about his folks in the past. "But his life choices have changed. He has you and little lady in there." I point a fry in the direction of her belly. "I'm sure they're ready to apologize and try to make up for lost time."

I can't imagine ever telling my child that I didn't want anything to do with them until they made decisions I wanted them to make. Thinking about Graham and the pain he felt at not being enough for his parents makes me feel protective—I want to tell them not to go. His parents don't deserve to have them in their lives now. But as I watch my daughter, I know they would be lucky to know her and her incredible husband.

"You're right. I'm apprehensive, but I told him I'd try to be polite." Shrugging her shoulders, she changes the subject. "So, have you heard from Gwen? I know as of Monday you still hadn't heard anything."

Shaking my head, I look at my phone, only to see a blank screen staring back at me. "No, but I can't fault her. I haven't reached out either."

Immediately, she scoffs at my admission. "You haven't texted or called her? Dad! Why not?"

My cheeks start to flush at her scolding me. "I know. I know. I've been giving her space. I kind of laid a lot of information out on the table at dinner. I might've frightened her." I take a bite and watch her.

Tessa tilts her head from side to side, as if she's thinking about how to word whatever she wants to say. "You men can be so daft sometimes. I'm going to leave, and you're either going to call her, or you're going to text her. Either way, you *are* going to reach out. Start with an apology for taking so long, and end with an invitation to dinner. Max can come hang out with Graham and I."

Without letting me respond, she's up and out the door.

I guess that's that then.

Me:

Hey Gwen, I'm sorry I haven't reached out sooner to check on you and Max. I hope everyone and everything is okay. I was wondering if you'd like to try to do dinner again sometime.

Me:

As a real date this time. Not a friend date.

I stare at the second message I sent with nerves raging in my stomach. Then I set my phone down and run my hand over my smooth head. Was that too forward with us both admitting we were scared of our feelings for each other? Will that scare her even more?

Chapter 14

Gwen

Relaxing in a bubble bath after an exhausting day of troubleshooting tablets and laptops that could easily have been fixed without my help, I look at my phone, reading and rereading the text I got from Paul at lunchtime.

He wants to take me on a date.

I wanted to tell him that I really wanted our dinner on Saturday to be a date, but I chickened out. Then everything with Max happened and I couldn't change my mind. But now, he's asking for a real date.

I set my phone on the edge of the tub and lean my head back on the bath pillow. I want to say yes to this date, but my nerves about Max are at the forefront of my mind. He says things are fine with Kyle, but I don't know if he's ready to go back over there while I go on a date. A date he would no doubt be against in the first place.

A chuckle escapes my mouth as I think about Max and his lack of subtlety when Paul is brought up in conversation, or when he was over helping me out. He means well, and I understand where he's coming from. Hell, I'm not sure if I'm quite ready to move on from his dad either. But I'll never know if I don't put myself out there to try.

After mulling it over, I grab my phone again so I can text Paul back. We're adults, I told him no games, so I'll be up-front.

Me:

I would love to, but I don't know how Max would feel staying home alone so soon after having a seizure.

Paul:

I've got that covered. Tessa said she and Graham would love to have him over. Graham has video games, or they could find something else to do. Possibly throw the ball around in the backyard?

Me:

Let me talk to him about it. If he agrees, then I'd love to go on a real date with you.

Relief and excitement crash through me after I hit send, all the while part of me instantly feels guilty and a bit nervous for agreeing. I swore I wouldn't allow myself to add any more people to my life that I could lose in a heartbeat, and accepting this invitation is like welcoming the inevitable heartbreak into my life.

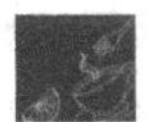

Max and I are lounging on the couch, his feet propped up on my lap, as we watch *Is It Cake?* and try to wrap our brains around the hyperrealism of this art. Turning my focus from the TV, I study him—his golden hair slightly in his eyes, his lip tucked between his teeth as he stares at the show. Every time I look at him, I'm reminded of Dwayne.

"Hey, bud, can I ask you something?" I say, pressing pause on the remote.

He shifts how he's sitting, pulling his legs into his body. "Yeah. What is it?" He rests his chin on top of his knees.

I take a deep breath as I collect my thoughts. "I know you don't like the idea of me dating right now. But—"

"No." He cuts me off before I can finish my train of thought. "You're right. I don't. And Dad wouldn't either." The features on his face harden as he stares at me.

"Well, that's where I'd have to disagree. Your father would want me to be happy—whatever that meant." I watch as his face drops, knowing I'm right. "Paul asked me out, and his daughter—you've met Tessa—and her husband have agreed to let you hang out at their place if you don't feel comfortable being home alone."

Max moves his feet to the floor and leans forward, arms resting on his knees. "And I don't have a say in whether or not you go on this date?" he asks, eyes holding mine.

I shake my head. "No, because I'm an adult and enjoy Paul's company. And quite frankly, I've been lonely. I miss your father more than words can explain, and I find comfort in knowing Paul can relate to that type of sadness."

He sighs as he stands up from the couch. "Well, I guess Tessa can babysit me while you go out. But, Mom . . ."

He pauses for a minute before he walks out of the room. "You might want to take your wedding rings off first."

My right hand automatically reaches for the ring set on my left finger. I haven't been able to bring myself to take them off. I've noticed at my LLGG meetings that other members have slowly been coming to sessions without their rings on. Each week it seems like another person has healed enough of themselves to take that step, and each week I wonder when—or if—I'll finally be able to do it.

Chapter 15

Paul

"**Y**ou are so cute," Tessa teases as I move the books on my coffee table for the third time.

I stand up and examine the living room again before meeting Tessa's gaze. "Why do you say that?" I ask, knowing damn well why she said it.

Her eyes glimmer as she smirks at me. "Dad, you moved those books *three* times. You are as nervous as one of Graham's middle school boys about to ask a girl to the school dance."

"Psh. I'm not nervous." I begin to pace, fighting the urge to bend down and move the books . . . again. I don't know why I just lied to Tess. She can very clearly see how nervous I am. Maybe admitting it out loud will make it worse.

"Keep telling yourself that, old man. Do you want any help worrying the carpet some more, or are you ready to sit down and eat?"

Letting out a huff, I walk into the kitchen and grab the napkins off the counter.

"But really, you have nothing to worry about. Gwen is great. You two have a lot in common and I've always wanted a sibling." She laughs as my face turns red at the mention of a sibling. "Joking! There's no pressure in marrying the woman, but a date will be good for you."

I incline my head as I pick up a slice of pizza. "You're right. I know you're right. But . . . *fuck*. This is nerve-racking."

She fidgets with her water bottle, watching me. "You know, I think I understand your fears. You've only ever been with Mom—she was your soulmate. But maybe we all get more than one soulmate in our lifetime? *I* personally never want to meet *my* other soulmate, but I like to think that maybe when Mom died she had a hand in putting Gwen in your path."

Closing my eyes, I can picture it—Sherri up in Heaven, sitting next to God, looking down on us and saying "*Her. She'd be perfect for him.*"

Opening my eyes, I smile at Tessa. "I like the thought of that."

I can't help but feel relieved that my therapist agreed to see me last minute—on a Saturday morning. As I'm leaving her office, I feel a little less anxious about my date this afternoon with Gwen. Dr. Milton and I spoke about my fears of going out with someone—feeling like I'm betraying Sherri and our wedding vows. She very kindly reminded me that Sherri literally told me to move on so I'm not forsaking either.

Gwen and I agreed on an afternoon date instead of an evening one to give us more time together instead of feeling rushed to get her back to Max. It's been a *very* long time since I've planned a first date so I keep second-guessing whether or not she'll like it. The plan is for Gwen to drop Max off with Tessa and Graham, then meet at my house where she'll leave her car for the duration of the day.

Driving down the road, I keep drumming my thumbs over the steering wheel to try to release the nervous energy buzzing through me. The low sounds of whatever hit country song is playing through my speaker gives noise to the otherwise quiet cab of my truck. "Stop feeling nervous. Sherri told you to find someone. You won't be able to do that without going out on a date," I say to myself as I pull into the driveway. "Besides, it's not like this is the first time you've spent time with Gwen. Get it together."

Last night at dinner, Tessa teased me about how on edge I am about today. I chuckle to myself as I recall her saying I'm acting like a middle schooler taking their crush out for the first time. Honestly, that's exactly how this feels. I want everything to be perfect and I'm scared she won't enjoy herself.

During our lunches the past two years we've discussed types of activities we like to do, as well as things neither one of us have done in a long time. While I was planning for this date, I was very thankful for those conversations.

Gwen sits at the table, playing with the string on her hoodie as I finish a phone call from work.

"Sorry about that. She needed to know where something was on my desk for a case she's working on." I tuck my phone in my front pocket.

She waves her hand in front of her face. "Don't worry about it . . . As I was saying, Max and I passed by a mini golf course the other day and I asked if he wanted to go some time. He said, and I quote, 'Like I would be caught dead doing that with my mom.' Needless to say, I haven't done any of those childhood activities I love so much." Her face falls as she recalls the conversation with Max.

"What do you consider childhood activities?" I ask, taking a sip of my root beer.

She taps her chin as she contemplates my question. "Mini golf, of course, bowling, the arcade, laser tag, the roller rink. Things that are typical for young teens to do with friends or on dates."

Nodding my head, I observe her as she continues to fidget with her hoodie. "The movies? Or is that not just for children and teens?"

"Oh, I love the movies, but I haven't gone in years. That's another one of those things where Max would rather stub his toe on a metal slab than go with me."

"Maybe you should ask Tessa if she'd like to go with you some time. She loves the movies and is always looking for an excuse to go." The thought of having her spend time with Tessa comes so easily.

Our conversation moves from activities we enjoy to books we've read recently and I can't help but think how easy this friendship feels. It doesn't seem like we've only known each other for a few months; it feels like we've been friends for years.

Gwen:

> *We're headed to Tessa's now. I should be at your place in fifteen minutes.*

Seeing Gwen's text lights a fire under my ass and gets me moving to finish getting ready. I quickly brush my teeth and rub sunscreen over my bald head. One thing I've become better at since losing my wife to cancer—putting skin protection on. She might not have had skin cancer, but I'll be damned if that gets me. As I make my way to the front of the house, I stop briefly to look at a picture of Tessa, Sherri, and I hanging on the wall.

"I'm going to try, baby. I'm going to try." I touch a finger to Sherri's bright smile before continuing to the door.

I'm locking the front door as Gwen is pulling her van next to my truck in the driveway. When she spots me, a grin breaks across her face, causing my heart to pound even quicker than it was before.

Walking over to her, I open the door before she gets a chance to do it herself. Her eyes sparkle as her smile grows wider, and I step back and take in her outfit. She's wearing high-waisted denim shorts with a burnt-orange, semi-casual tank top tucked in, showcasing her curvy figure. Her hair is in a ponytail—her purple ribbon tattoo on display—and she has on a pair of white sneakers. I smile appreciatively at her take on my "dress for comfort" request.

Leaning in, I greet her with a hug and a brief kiss on the cheek. "You look nice," I comment as I pull away.

"Thanks, you do too." Her eyes travel the length of my body as a slight pink creeps across her cheeks.

I've got on a pair of jeans, a sunflower-yellow Henley that Tessa got me for Christmas, and a pair of brown boots. Nothing fancy, but the way she takes me in makes my own face heat. Tessa was right. I'm as nervous as a teenager going on their first date.

"Are you ready to go?" I ask, snapping out of my thoughts.

Gwen nods her head with a sheepish smile, and I walk the few steps to my truck so I can open the passenger door for her. Holding out my hand, I help her climb into the cab.

"So, where are we going?" she asks as I take my seat behind the wheel and pull my seatbelt on.

Smiling, I turn to look at her before I answer. "I thought we'd go play mini golf and eat at the little cafeteria they have there. If that sounds good to you?"

I watch her face for any sign of disappointment at my plans. Instead, her head whips up and she squeals like a little kid on Christmas opening their most anticipated gift. "Are we really?"

When I nod in response, she bounces in her seat and claps her hands before buckling herself in. Her joy warms my chest.

"What are you waiting for? We've got mini golf to play!" she says, patting the dashboard in front of her.

Chapter 16

Gwen

The pure excitement I feel over the fact that Paul is taking us to play mini golf washes away any residual nerves I still felt from this morning. I've wanted to play mini golf for so long but haven't had anyone to go with, and I feel weird going to places like this by myself.

We're standing in line behind a young couple who's probably Max's age, and I feel like I should be embarrassed, but it just makes me that much happier. Being out on a date—a *real* date—makes me feel young again, so it only feels right to be around people who are young too.

When it's our turn at the ticket counter, the teenage girl smiles at us. "Good afternoon! How many are in your group?"

"Good afternoon. Just the two of us today." Paul looks at me, smiling and lifting his eyebrows.

"That'll be twenty-two fifty," the girl says, the smile still plastered on her face.

I glance around the mini golf course as Paul pays and grabs the clubs and balls we'll be using. Families and groups of teenagers are scattered throughout, laughing at their conversations and each other. My smile widens as butterflies resume flapping in my stomach.

"So, would you like to play the course first, or grab a bite to eat at the food court?" Paul asks, as I turn my attention back to him.

Taking my lower lip between my teeth, I survey our surroundings. The food court looks less crowded at the moment, and as I turn to check out the course my stomach lets out a rumble. "Sounds like we should probably grab something to eat first." I laugh, putting my hand over my growling belly.

He takes the golf clubs in one hand, sticks the balls in his pocket, and places his other hand on my lower back as he leads the way to the line. We stand a few paces away from the counter as we peruse the menu, and my mind homes in on his hand still resting on my lower back instead of trying to decide what to order. The slight contact sends a wave of contentment and desire through me.

"Do you know what you want?" Paul asks, leaning closer to my ear.

I nod as I inhale deeply, the scent of his minty breath and sunscreen more intoxicating than it has any right being. "I think I want a corndog, some fries, and maybe a funnel cake." His eyes light up as I mention the fried doughy goodness.

As soon as we've gotten our food and are sitting down, I start to feel nervous again. We've spent many hours together eating and getting to know each other, but never in this context. I'm not even sure what we're supposed to talk about.

Luckily, Paul seems to have come prepared because he jumps right in. "I know this is a first date and some topics are typically off the table, but we're both adults who've been married before, so I feel like we should be able to talk about whatever we want."

I blink at him a bit, confused as to where this conversation is headed.

He clears his throat before he continues. "What I mean is, people typically stay away from discussing past relationships on the first date. But our past relationships have shaped and molded us into who we are today, and I think it's important that we don't shy away from those topics. I want you to feel comfortable asking me anything about my past—with Sherri or without. Though, if I'm being honest, more than most of my history has to do with her. We got together in high school, after all."

Nodding, I pick up my corndog and dip it in mustard. "Is there a question you wanted to ask that you're afraid I might not be comfortable answering? Or are you afraid I have a question I thought you might be uncomfortable answering?" I ask, amused at how flustered he seems to have gotten while going on his spiel.

His cheeks turn a shade darker as he thinks of his answer. "Well, it's just that I don't think we can avoid talking about our late spouses while getting to know each other better. I don't want you to feel like you can't talk about him—Dwayne, that is. I will always want to hear whatever you'd like to share."

Chewing my food, I think about what he's saying. I can't help but notice how cute he is when he's nervous. "Okay. So, how about we get questions about them out of the way. We know the basics from what we've shared about them in group and lunches, but is there anything else you'd like to know?"

"How about I start easy? Why don't you tell me your favorite memory you have with him?" he asks, eyes locked on me.

My lip lifts up in the corner as my mind instantly takes me back to when I was twenty-three.

"I can't believe your sister invited us here for the weekend and then ditched us," Dwayne says, laughing as we climb into a cab, getting us off the streets of Columbus.

I roll my eyes as he leans forward to tell the cab driver the hotel we're staying at. "We knew it was a possibility. Brandi's finishing up nursing school and told us she might have to pick up a shift at the hospital." He's acting as if us coming out here isn't going to turn into a nice getaway now that we don't have to actually visit with my twin.

"I guess you're right. And we never did get a honeymoon. We can treat this weekend like one," he says, leaning in to nuzzle my neck.

I tilt my head up, granting access for him to rub his stubbly face against my delicate skin. I let out a soft moan mixed with a giggle at the sensation. "Why don't we hold off on this until we've made it back to the room, Cowboy." I chuckle and slowly lift my shoulder, effectively putting a stop to the kisses, causing him to groan in displeasure.

"Fine. But I get to pick what we do today," Dwayne says, resting his hand on my thigh and smiling at me with a roguish look on his face.

"Fishing? That's what you wanted to do today?" I ask as he hands me one of the fishing poles he rented from a rental business next to the Scioto River.

His laugh sends a delicious shiver down my body, making me excited to get him back to our room. "You love fishing, Gwen. We went fishing on our first date."

He has a point, but this is not what I thought he had in mind for the day.

We spend a few hours fishing before returning our poles as the sun begins to set. Grabbing my hand, he leads me down the sidewalk toward downtown. "I also thought you might like to go on a ghost tour. Brandi said there are a few really good ones here."

I stop in my tracks as he pulls my hand up to his mouth, kissing it. "What?" he asks.

"Dwayne Bryant Waters, are you recreating our first date?" I ask with tears pricking my eyes.

A playful smile cracks his face. "Maybe . . . If you keep walking, you can find out." He softly pulls on my hand to get me moving again.

By the time the ghost tour is finished, the only place open is a small pizza restaurant, which coincidentally, is what we had on our first date. We order a large pie to go with everything on it and walk back to the hotel.

The rest of the weekend is a blur of body parts in positions that would make my mom blush, and cuddling while we dream about what our future will look like.

By the time I'm done sharing my favorite memory, Paul is no longer sitting across from me, he's in the booth next to me with his arm wrapped around me. Comforting me, I realize, as I feel tears slide down my cheeks.

Chapter 17

Paul

It was instinct that urged me to move so I could comfort her the moment her voice started to crack. If I knew asking her favorite memory would trigger such powerful emotions, I wouldn't have asked about it in the food court of a mini golf course.

Gwen wipes at her eyes as she leans into my embrace. "I'm sorry for crying. It's been a while since I thought about that weekend, much less talked about it. I got pregnant that trip, but miscarried. Nobody but Dwayne and I knew about it."

I tighten my grip around her shoulder. "I'm so sorry. We can talk about anything else." I rest my chin against her head, resisting the urge to place a kiss on her forehead.

She takes in a shuddering breath before pulling herself from my arms. I watch as she wipes at her eyes a few more times before picking up her Cherry Coke. Her posture shifts slightly before she turns her body so she's facing me, legs tucked under her. "What made you decide to join LLGG?"

A bit taken aback by this particular change in topic, I bite the inside of my cheek. I did tell her we could talk about anything else, but the answer isn't that I had some huge revelation. It doesn't even really feel worth mentioning, but it's her question.

"When Sherri was first diagnosed with cancer, my mental health started to take a dive. I was going to work but I wasn't fully focused. And being a cop, that's a huge issue." I take a breath as I recall the moment Sherri suggested therapy. "Coming to the realization that I was going to lose my best friend of thirty-something years was hard. She could tell that I was in a bad place, and I think she was tired of having to be strong for me too . . ." I scrunch my eyebrows, trying to find the words to explain this correctly. "Not tired in the sense of being annoyed, but tired in the sense that it was starting to become too taxing. So she encouraged me to start seeing a therapist."

Gwen's blue eyes are focused on my hands as I absentmindedly fidget with the plastic fork on my plate. She uses her knee to nudge me, letting me know she's here, listening, when I'm ready to continue.

"A few visits after she passed, Dr. Milton—my therapist—said she thought it would be good for me to talk to other people who have also gone through the experience of losing someone. She mentioned a few different groups, but only one was specific to losing one's spouse. Once I went to my first meeting, I met some really great people, so I decided to continue going." I look at her with a small smile. If anyone can understand the comfort of those meetings, it's Gwen.

She places her hand on my thigh and gives it a gentle squeeze. "Well, I'm very thankful for Dr. Milton then. Without that suggestion, we would've never met." Her smile is bright as her eyes bounce between mine.

We finish eating our lunch and move to lighter topics: favorite bands, foods, TV shows, and books. After I take my last bite, she pushes my knee with the hand that somehow never left my leg the whole time. "Are you ready to go get your ass handed to you?"

"Oh, you are so on," I say, standing and reaching out to help her up.

As we make our way through the course, our conversations stay in, what I imagine is, first date territory. "When did you decide you wanted to become a cop?" Gwen asks, setting her club up to hit the ball.

"Honestly, I don't remember ever wanting to be anything else. My parents have pictures of me as young as three pretending to be a police officer. I've been told many stories about how I bribed my sister into being the bad guy so I could arrest her."

Gwen lets out a snort then immediately covers her mouth and starts laughing harder. "Oh shit. That was unattractive." She holds her hand up as she collects herself before continuing. "But really, that is so adorable. You'll have to show me those pictures one day."

My heart starts playing hopscotch in my chest at the thought of there being *one day* where I can show her pictures from my childhood. "What about you? Did you always want to be in engineering? And did your engineering job in Lancer look similar to what it does now?"

"No. I originally wanted to go to culinary school. But even though I enjoy cooking—and am pretty good at it—I decided I didn't want to risk falling out of love with a hobby that brought me so much joy. So, in college, I took a few random low-level classes that mostly led down the engineering path and really liked them." Her eyes meet mine as we walk to the next hole. "I'm really good at math, even though you wouldn't be able to tell—not with how shitty I am at finances. And no, I was actually in a lab back in Lancer, working with my hands and building things. Now I'm basically glorified IT—fixing electronics that end up messing up one way or the other."

Before I know it, we're on the eighteenth hole and I'm losing. In hopes of distracting Gwen, I start singing—horribly—to the pop music playing over the speakers. Her knees slightly bend, gaze intense on the ball as she holds the putter in her hands. My voice gets louder as the chorus plays words I actually know, and I see the moment her concentration breaks as a smile tugs at the corner of her mouth. She swings at the ball, and it rolls across the green before it bounces against the wall, causing it to slide right back to where it started.

I whoop in a childish act of victory for making her mess up on her turn. However, my excitement dies quickly when I look at her and find her glaring at me. My cheeks flush as I lower my head in apology.

"Oh no, don't look ashamed now, Lord Gaga. Please, continue singing." A smile forms on her face as she tries to maintain a stern tone.

I watch her face, assessing to see if I really screwed up by distracting her. Her face is unreadable, though, aside from the grin she's trying to suppress. But people respond to anger in various ways, and I'm unsure if this is an angry smile or an amused smile.

"Your turn," she says, gesturing to the front of the hole and moving out of the way.

Nodding, I take a tentative step forward before placing my ball down. I close my eyes as I inhale and relax my shoulders as I prepare myself for the final round. If I can make it on the first try, I can walk away with some dignity.

The moment I swing the putter back Gwen starts singing along to the song that just started playing, at the top of her lungs. Surprised by the unexpected sound, I hit the ball so hard it pops out of the course and into the small stream. I slowly turn around to face Gwen and see her doubled over in laughter—unbridled snorting and tears falling down her cheeks. The sight makes my knees weak and the sound makes my heart pound.

Chapter 18

Gwen

I haven't laughed like this in years, and it feels so good to be able to be carefree for a little bit. I glance up at Paul who has started laughing while looking at the stream and rubbing his hand over his head. I blink to clear the tears that have formed from my amusement.

"Well, do you suppose I tell them the ball went into the water, or do I try to fish it out myself?" Paul asks, walking to the edge of the faux grass.

Taking the few steps needed to stand next to him, I peer into the water. Seeing his red ball at the bottom, among other lost balls, causes me to wheeze.

"I think it's safe to say you don't need to get it yourself. It looks like it has friends." I force myself to take a deep breath to calm down. Losing that war, I start laughing some more.

His cheeks deepen a shade with what might be embarrassment, but could also be enjoyment. Then, he chuckles as he turns to face me. "I guess there's no way I can come back and beat you now without a ball."

With that, I make a show of strutting to my yellow ball and getting my putter in position. I keep my eyes trained on him as I tap the ball. Neither of us breaks eye contact until we hear the subtle clink of my ball falling into the hole. Paul's eyes slowly leave mine so he can look into the hole. They slightly widen when he sees that it did, in fact, go in.

His lip lifts up, a smirk forming on his face. Dropping the putter, he takes two large strides before standing directly in front of me. His hands go to my jaw, and with a quick survey of my eyes, he leans down, claiming my mouth with his.

Instinctively, I drop my putter, my hands finding their way around his neck, pulling him deeper into the kiss. My lips open, allowing his tongue to sweep in and dance with mine, and a muffled moan leaves my body. I'm not typically one who enjoys public displays of affection, but this kiss is . . . intoxicating.

The sound of girlish giggles causes us to break apart. I turn my head, placing my lips against my shoulder as I take in a group of five teenage girls watching us and snickering with each other. Unable to find it in me to be embarrassed, I grab Paul's hand, bend down to grab my golf club, walk over to pick up his abandoned putter, and nod my head at the girls as we pass by.

"Ladies," Paul says, before leading the way to the exit.

When we get to Paul's house, I bounce on my toes as I wait for him to unlock the door. I feel like a teenager—giddy anticipation coursing through my body. As soon as the door is open, we come together, kissing clumsily and he leads us to his room. He awkwardly steps out of his shoes while his fingers are tangled in my hair and his lips are on my neck. I follow his lead, and we leave a trail of discarded shoes along the hallway.

When we reach his room, I pull back and take in his kiss-swollen lips. As his stare burns a hole into mine, I take off my shirt and toss it aside. Licking my lips, I watch as he echoes my movements and loses his shirt. Then he reaches forward to grab the button on my shorts but hesitates before it unclasps.

Paul's blue eyes meet mine. "Is this what you want?" he asks, voice laced with desire.

I nod my head and let out a breathy response. "More than anything. You?"

"Fuck yes," he says, pulling me into him by the top of my pants, his lips crashing down on mine as our bodies collide.

My fingers deftly undo his belt, button, and zipper, and at the same time, he manages to rid me of my shorts. Then he turns us around and lowers me onto the bed. His pupils are blown as he takes me in.

I move my arms over my stomach, a moment of panic rushing through me. My stretch marks from carrying Max for nine months, the scar from my c-section and ultimate hysterectomy—all of it causes a mild anxiety to sweep into my brain. I haven't been on display like this since Dwayne, and all of a sudden it feels like too much.

Sensing my unease, Paul kneels in front of me. "Hey, what's wrong?" His voice is so tender, my heart cracks a little.

My vision blurs as tears pool in my eyes. Great, the second time I've cried on this date—third if you count when I was laughing. I take in a shuddering breath and count to four before letting it out.

"It's just . . . It's been a while since I've been with anyone, and nobody besides Dwayne has seen my body post-Max." I force myself to look at Paul's face. "The stretch marks. The scar. It's a little more anxiety-inducing than I anticipated," I admit. *Honesty.*

He takes my hand and watches me, making sure I'm paying attention to him before he speaks. "This body is perfect. It brought your child into this world." He kisses my hand. "It houses your caring heart and your brilliant brain." He kisses my forehead and taps my chest. "And this scar? It just means you went through a pretty terrifying delivery . . . and survived." He leans down and places a kiss right at the top of my panties, on the soft skin where my jagged scar rests. "Don't ever feel embarrassed about how you look. You are beautiful."

Now my tears are falling in earnest because of his words. I nod my head and pull him up next to me. When he's seated on the bed, I push on his chest slightly, guiding him to lie back.

Once he's scooted himself up and is lying back on his bed, I tug at his briefs. He lifts his hips and uses his hands to help take them off, and I watch as his impressive length bobs free from its prison.

"Do I need a condom?" he asks, a hint of apprehension in his voice.

I shake my head. "I got a hysterectomy—no more kids for me. And like I mentioned, I haven't been with anyone since Dwayne. But if you prefer—"

He cuts me off. "No. No, I haven't been with anyone since Sherri either."

A smile tugs on my lips as I nod in understanding. I sit up on my knees and wiggle out of my panties before straddling his legs. He sits up and reaches behind my back, unclasping my bra. My heavy breasts fall with the loss of support.

Paul sucks in a breath right before he leans forward and sucks one of my nipples into his mouth. My head lolls back and I let out a moan. He wraps his arms around my waist and pulls my body closer to him, his erection hard and slightly pulsing between us.

I lift myself up on my knees and take his cock into one hand. I stroke him for a few seconds while I use my other hand to play with my clit. I might be turned on, but I don't think I'm wet enough to take him yet.

Watching my movements closely, Paul moves my hand out of the way and slowly picks up where I left off. I work my hand up and down his shaft as he works his fingers over my clit and into my pussy. I feel the wetness gather at my center as he pumps his fingers deeper and circles his thumb quicker.

Quickly stopping him, I adjust myself, lining the head of his cock up with my slit. My thumb rubs the bead of pre-cum over the tip before I gradually lower onto him. He lets out a deep husky groan as my pussy slides onto him, and my hands land on his chest, pushing him back against the bed as I slowly twist my hips.

Once I'm fully seated on him, I take a moment to feel the way he stretches me. All the while, Paul lies with his head on the pillow, gaze glued to where our bodies are connected. Smiling, my eyes flick down too as his thumb makes its way to my clit.

Chapter 19

Paul

Fuck, the sight of Gwen on top of me is one of the sexiest things I've ever seen. Her blonde ponytail grazes the top of her shoulder as she slowly starts bouncing on my cock, and my free hand roams up her thigh and to her waist where I gently squeeze. I watch her face as her eyes become hooded and her head tilts backward.

"Holy . . . shit. You feel so fucking good inside me," she pants, picking up speed.

I let out a soft chuckle. "I was just thinking a very similar thought. Your pussy is so tight, it feels incredible. I'm a little embarrassed to admit, but this might not last long." I try not to cringe outwardly at the admission, but it's been a long two years and this feels too fucking good.

My thumb traces circles over her clit as her body grinds against mine. I feel the walls of her pussy start to clench around my cock and her breathing becomes erratic.

"Breathe, Gwen," I say as her body stiffens, her orgasm pulling her under.

She continues twisting lazily on my lap as she comes down from her orgasm, and I put my hands on her hips, bringing her to a stop.

Her eyes snap open. "What are you doing?" she asks, trying to wiggle again.

"Let's switch positions. Roll over on your back," I suggest, but she shakes her head, climbing off me anyway.

Suddenly, my cock is met with the cold air of the room leaving me slightly confused, until I see her bend forward, bracing herself on her forearms. Her ass is in the air, swollen pink pussy on display—her cum glistening in the light—causing my dick to stand at attention.

"Are you just going to sit there and stare?" Gwen asks in a sultry voice I haven't heard from her before.

Wasting no time, I get up on my knees and kneel behind her. I line myself up with her opening and slide in effortlessly. As my body presses against her ass, she lets out a mewl of pleasure.

Then Gwen lets out another moan. "Fuck, yes. Right there. Can you play with my clit again?"

Loving that she asks for what she wants, I reach around her body and use my middle finger to rub where she asked. I quickly get lost in the rhythm of my hips thrusting back and forth and the sound of my balls smacking against her.

I feel her pussy tighten around me again as her body prepares for another orgasm. This time, as I feel her reach her release, I don't hold back when my balls send the signal to my brain and a tremor runs through my spine, pumping two more times before spilling into her and pulling out, finishing on the bed.

Gwen rolls over to her side, bringing her arm up to rest her head in her hand.

Leaning forward, I plant a kiss on her lips. "I'll be right back," I say, jumping out of the bed and jogging to the bathroom.

When I get into the bathroom, I grab a washcloth and put soap on it. I quickly clean myself off before grabbing a second washcloth to clean Gwen with. Making my way back to the bed, I smile as she watches me intently. I hold up the damp cloth before she reaches for it.

"Uh uh. I made the mess, I'll clean it up." Crouching between her legs, I softly rub the material over the inside of her thighs before folding it and moving to her pussy, cleaning both of our releases from her body.

When we get to Gwen's car, I can't help but already miss her. The thought scares me, though, and I can't help but question if it's her or the intimacy we just shared that I'll miss. Surely it's too soon since losing Sherri for me to feel this attached to another woman.

I stand in front of Gwen, holding her hand, my thumb rubbing along the outside of her wrist. "I had a fun time mini golfing, and even more fun after."

Her cheeks pinken at my comment. "I had a great time too. The whole day is one I'll remember forever. And if

I still kept a diary, I would probably write about it as soon as I got home, with your name surrounded by little hearts," she says, a lightness in her voice. "Well, I should probably go pick Max up. He'll no doubt be complaining about how he had to be *babysat* today." Rolling her eyes, she smiles at me.

I nod my head once and then lean in to kiss her. "Drive safe on the way home, and please text me to let me know you made it safely."

She responds with another smile and a tilt of her head before turning to get in her van.

Chapter 20

Gwen

Max is quiet as we drive home from Tessa and Graham's house. He only said a few words as he climbed into the front seat, but Tessa assured me that he was a great guest and told him he was welcome to come over whenever he felt like hanging out.

"So, did you have fun with Tessa and Graham?" I ask, trying to break the silence.

Nodding his head and grunting is his only form of acknowledgement as he continues staring out the window. I purse my lips as I think of another way to get him to talk.

"What'd you guys do?" I attempt an open-ended question, hoping to get more than what resembles a mutter. I peer at him out of the corner of my eye as I pull into the driveway, and he lifts his shoulder in response.

Before I can say anything else, he opens the door and takes off toward the house. " What's his deal?" I question the empty car.

Pulling out my cell phone before I go inside, I send Paul a text.

> *Made it home. Thank you again for an in-credible afternoon. I hope we can do it again soon.*

I type and erase a heart emoji, then a winking face, and then a kissing face before deciding not to add one. As soon as that's done I make my way to the front door and see Max sitting on the step instead of having used his key to get inside.

"Did you have fun?" he asks, looking down at the scuffed up shoes he refuses to let me toss.

Hesitating, I sit beside him. I don't want to lie to him, but I don't want him to think I'm trying to replace his father either. Looking up at the lone dogwood tree in the front yard I let out a sigh. "I did. He took me to play mini golf."

He lets out a small laugh. "Mini golf is for kids." Looking at me, he must see something in my eyes, because he adds, "But I know you've been wanting to go, so I'm glad he took you somewhere you enjoyed."

Nudging his shoulder with my own, I say, "So, do you want to tell me why I got the silent treatment all the way home?" Turning to look at him, I expect him to roll his eyes and brush off my question.

"You took them off," Max says so quietly I almost don't hear him.

My brows furrow as I try to decipher what he's talking about. I look down at my body to see if I forgot to put something back on at Paul's house.

Noticing my confusion he gets a little louder. "Your rings. I told you that you should take them off. I guess I didn't think you'd actually do it." His admission makes me take a deep breath.

"You noticed that, did you?" I play with my left ring finger where my wedding set used to be.

"I don't want you to start dating someone and forget about Dad." His voice cracks as he speaks.

The next thing out of his mouth catches me by surprise and has me confused.

"Sometimes I really hate myself." Tears leak from his eyes as he talks.

"What are you talking about, baby?" I turn my whole body and pull him into my embrace.

"If I hadn't caused that car accident, he'd still be here. If my body didn't decide to fuck up and make me have a seizure, I wouldn't have crashed." His body shakes as he sobs in my arms. "And sometimes I get mad at him for agreeing to take me driving that day. I *just* got my permit! Why did he have to let me drive so soon?"

Tears are falling down my face as I hold my weeping son. "Baby," I say, trying to get his attention. "Maxwell, listen to me."

He lifts his head so his glassy eyes are looking at me.

"I don't know what made you start thinking about this, but it is *not* your fault that your father died. Yes, your seizure caused the accident, but you'd never had one before. How could you or he have known not to let you get behind that wheel?" I'm rubbing my hands along his back, comforting him as he releases these emotions.

"I would have taken you out if he didn't offer. Baby, you are not at fault, and I don't like that you're blaming yourself. How long have you felt this way?" I pull back from him—just slightly—so I can look at his face better.

He takes his arm and rubs his snotty nose along the back. "Since I heard the news that he died on impact." That single piece of information breaks my heart. He's been living with this guilt for two years—blaming himself for the death of his dad. I wrap my arms around him even tighter than before, tears quietly gliding down my cheeks and onto my neck.

Chapter 21

Paul

Pulling into the police station, I reach for my phone as soon as I'm parked. I typically have Sundays off—or work the night shift—so I can go to church and then group. However, the chief called me in for a meeting this morning, so even though it's supposed to be a day off, I'm here.

Me:

> *I won't be at the meeting today, got called into work. Hopefully we can see each other soon.*

Gwen:

> *Okay. Is everything okay?*

Me:

> *He didn't say, but I hope so.*

"Good, you're here," Chief Elgin says as I knock on his door. "Please, take a seat. I don't have long before everyone starts showing up." He gestures to a seat in front of his desk.

Sitting down, I don't say anything because he's a straight-to-the-point type of man, and I know he'll get to the reason he called me in a moment. Instead, I take in his office and notice that his walls are bare in comparison to the last time I was here.

"Paul, I'm retiring," he states. "You've put in the man-hours, you're well-respected, and have great rapport with the ladies and gentlemen that work here. I think it's time we drop the deputy in front of your title and make you chief. What do you say?" He stands up, walking around his desk, and leans against it as he waits for my response.

Chief. I've wanted this position for years now, but I didn't think it would happen. I think back to the letter Sherri wrote me . . . She believed in me and knew this day would come.

"I'd be honored to take your place as Chief of Police, sir," I say, standing up and reaching my hand toward his outstretched one.

"Perfect. Now, let's go let the precinct know." Dropping my hand, he walks to the door and leaves me to follow behind him.

Chief Elgin walks into the bullpen, where the precinct is buzzing with life. Some cops are nose deep in case files, others are talking on the phone, while some are lounging back, talking to their buddies at the desk next to them.

He moves to the middle of the room and clears his throat to get everyone's attention. Looking around, he waits while phones are hung up and folders are set aside.

"I'm sure many of you have heard the whispers, and it's about time I put them to rest. I am indeed retiring next month." There are a few people who let out surprised gasps—they clearly didn't hear the rumors. A few murmurs start as Chief Elgin takes a moment before continuing.

"Paul Gunter will be taking my place. He has been an excellent deputy chief and I fully believe he'll be the perfect replacement for me. Everyone, please, let's congratulate Paul on a job well done." He motions toward me and everyone starts clapping.

My buddy Larry walks over, giving me a hug. "Congratulations, Pauly. Sherri would be so proud of you," he says, loud enough for only me to hear. I smile and my chest warms.

She would be proud of me.

After the meeting disperses, people walk up, shaking my hand and offering me congratulations. When the crowd thins out and everyone returns to their work, I say my goodbyes and head back out to my truck. There are a few people I need to talk to.

Me:

Got some news. Can I come over?

Tessa:

Since when do you ask before coming over?

Graham:

You're always welcome.

My immediate thought when Elgin offered me the promotion was, *I need to tell Tess.* My second thought? *I need to tell Gwen.* That second thought has me feeling a little scared, though. Is it too soon to *want* to share my good news with her?

I ponder my feelings as I make the twenty-minute drive to my neighborhood. Parking in my driveway, I walk a few houses down before knocking on my daughter's door.

"Hey, Dad," she greets, with a hug and a kiss to my cheek. "Come on in. I was just about to make a plate of chicken Alfredo, would you like some?"

I blanche. "Who made it?"

Tessa's eyes narrow when she looks at me. "That was *one* time! And it was over two years ago!"

Graham's laugh booms from the kitchen as he calls out, "I made it. But she's getting better!"

Tessa places her hand on her belly and turns away from me, waddling to the kitchen and mumbling to herself about garlic cloves and minced garlic. When we reach the kitchen, I lean down to pick up their tuxedo cat, Catsby, and scratch behind his ears.

"Hey, Paul. So . . . would you like some?" Graham asks, holding a plate of chicken Alfredo out to Tessa.

Peeking over his shoulder into the pot, I nod my head, and he turns around to fix both of us plates before setting them down on the table. I set Catsby back down to wash my hands before sitting down next to Tessa. We sit there, watching as her husband walks to the fridge, grabbing us drinks.

"Okay, Dad. What's the news?" Tessa asks without waiting for Graham to take a seat.

Once Graham is seated, I twirl some pasta on my fork, taking a bite before jumping into the announcement. Her eyes narrow at me, causing Graham to laugh.

I take a deep breath, my gaze bouncing between the two of them as they sit, anxiously waiting. "I got a promotion. You are eating lunch with the unofficial, new Chief of Police." I smile broadly at them as Tessa squeals and jumps out of her seat.

"Really? Daddy, that's such great news!" She wraps her arms around me and I feel her body shake before I hear her sniffle in my ear—pregnancy hormones getting the best of her. "Mom would be so proud."

Chapter 22

Gwen

It's late—almost eleven at night. I texted Paul at eight asking if he wanted to come over, and his response was immediate. Now, we're sitting on the tailgate of his truck, talking about our day.

"How was that meeting with your boss?" I finally ask. I swing my legs as they dangle off the edge as I wait for him to answer.

He runs his hand over his head and grips the back of his neck before he turns to face me. The movement puts me on alert, making me a little nervous about what he has to say.

"It was great, actually. The chief is retiring and he wants me to take his spot." His smile spreads wide across his face, making his crow's-feet deepen.

I gasp excitedly and jump into his space, throwing my arms around him. "Paul! That's fantastic! You've talked about wanting to become chief for as long as I've known you." My excitement causes my voice to increase a few octaves.

He lets out a deep chuckle as he returns my hug, and my body instantly relaxes into his embrace. Loosening my arms, I pull back before asking, "How did Tessa react? I'm assuming she's the first person you told."

"A lot like you. Except, there may have been tears—hers, not mine." His hand rests on my leg as he shares the story of receiving the news. The heat of his palm reaching me beneath my yoga pants and scorching my leg in the most comforting way.

We sit in my driveway for another hour, talking about our plans for the week before Paul tells me I should head in and sleep. Reluctantly, I agree. Paul hops off the tailgate then holds out his hand to help me down. Keeping hold of my hand, he leads me to my porch. I'm not sure why, but I expected to part ways at the door of his truck.

When we reach the front door, I pause briefly before opening it. "Thank you for coming over tonight. It wouldn't have felt like a Sunday if I didn't get to see you." I don't give him time to respond before I step on my tiptoes and gently kiss his lips.

I pull back less than an inch before Paul places his hands on my neck, guiding me back to him. His kiss is passionate and firm, demanding and warm. My knees feel weak the longer our kiss goes on.

Paul breaks the kiss and leans his forehead against mine. "Thanks for inviting me over. Have a wonderful night, Gwen. Sleep well and have sweet dreams." He plants a quick kiss on my lips again before he turns around, heading for his truck.

Thursday afternoon, I'm taking my lunch at the park across from my office, enjoying the cool April weather before the summer heat takes over. My mind replays this past weekend with Paul, and though I feel butterflies when I think about it, I also get hit with an overwhelming sense of uncertainty.

"Dwayne, I don't know what to do," I say aloud, addressing my deceased husband. "I promised myself I wouldn't let anyone else in. I have Max and he's always been enough, and I don't know if my heart can take letting someone else in and then something happening to them. But . . . there's just something so centering about Paul. He makes me feel a lot like you did."

Taking a bite of my tuna sandwich, I look up at the towering maple tree standing in front of the picnic table. "I just wish I knew what to do," I say quietly to myself.

As I go to pick up my can of Dr. Pepper, I catch sight of a flash of red in the tree. Taking a sip, I squint my eyes, watching as a vibrant red cardinal hops along a branch, looking at me. I stop moving and stare at the beautiful bird. It feels as if we're having a staring contest—he doesn't turn his head or so much as ruffle a feather.

After long moments of the cardinal surveying me, I observe him as he flies away. A sense of calm resolve washes through me as I watch him disappear into the sky.

Chapter 23

Paul

It's been a little over a week since news of my promotion and I've had to be at work more than usual to prepare for the shift. Due to my hectic schedule, I haven't had time to see Gwen, but I spend my free time texting her, and we've had a few late night phone calls.

The day is dragging by as I sit in my office going over paperwork one of the detectives dropped off. Looking at the clock, I wince as I notice the time. It's already one-thirty; I planned on surprising Graham with lunch today. Good thing he wasn't aware of my plans so I didn't leave him in a lurch.

"You're still here?" my buddy Larry says, popping his head in my office.

Larry and I went through the police academy together and were lucky enough to have both found permanent homes here at MPD. He steps in and takes a seat.

Exhaling a heavy breath, I hold up the file I'm looking at. "Fritz dropped this off on her way out. I have a few things to look over before I can leave."

He nods his head in understanding. Then he leans forward, grabbing a picture frame from my desk. It's a picture of Sherri and I at my graduation from the academy. We were young—newlyweds at the time. My heart feels heavy with grief as he stares at the picture. Larry was with me when I got the phone call from Tessa telling me that Sherri passed away in her sleep.

"She really would be so damn proud of you," he says, placing the frame back down.

We sit there in silence, memories of Sherri flooding my mind.

"That was a really good answer. I honestly didn't know what you would say to that question," Sherri says, laughing as she sets aside a question card.

She's been helping me study for the instructional portion of the police academy exams every night without question. When I come home bone tired after the exhaustive work from the physical training we go through, Sherri always has dinner on the table and a smile on her face as she asks about my day.

Once dinner is through, she picks up the deck of study cards she created and helps me with the academic portion. She's always been the brains in the relationship—first my English tutor in high school, now making sure I'm prepared for the police academy.

"You really didn't have an inkling as to how I would handle having to pull over a family member?" I laugh as she shrugs.

"I thought if you pulled me over you'd punish me at home." She bats her eyes and bites her lip.

I drop the stack of cards I was holding and lunge toward her, causing my favorite sound to escape her mouth. "Oh, I'll punish you all right!" I say, nibbling on her ear and moving my hand beneath her pajama bottoms.

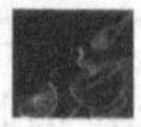

"All that studying paid off!" Sherri exclaims, jumping into my arms after my graduation ceremony. "How bad do you think those handcuffs will hurt when I let you cuff me to the bed?" Her voice is quiet in my ear.

I choke out a laugh as I look over at my parents to make sure they didn't hear. But my mom and dad are just standing there, beaming at me. My mom holds her camera up and motions to Sherri and I. "Okay you two, look over here so I can capture this moment!"

Sherri doesn't take her eyes off me as the camera flashes. Glancing down at her once my mom lowers her camera, I see her big brown eyes are filled with so much love and admiration.

"I can't wait for the rest of our lives, Officer Gunter." She reaches up and plants a kiss on my cheek.

As soon as I'm about to start a conversation with Larry, my phone buzzes, the name on the screen eliciting a goofy-ass grin on my face.

"Who's got you smiling like that?" he teases, feigning like he's going to grab my phone.

I feel heat creep up my neck and onto my face. "I've been seeing this woman," I admit, a pang of guilt in my chest warring with the flutters of butterflies in my stomach at the mention of Gwen.

A knowing smirk pulls on his lips. "If she's got you looking like a schoolboy just from glimpsing a text, I'm sure Sherri would approve."

There it is, that niggle of guilt rearing its head again. I force a smile on my face and give a brief nod. The look I give him must indicate that I'd like to be alone with my conflicting thoughts, though, because Larry stands up, dismissing himself with a wave.

After work I take the short thirty-minute drive out to Sherri's lake. One of the only spots in town—aside from the home we shared—that makes me feel like I can actually feel her presence. I stopped at Zigglers on the way to grab a sandwich and a sweet tea. I can't explain it, but the desire to bring her favorite meal today felt strong.

Walking out to the bench at the end of the dock, I look around at the tall maple and pine trees casting shade over the lake.

"Hey, Sher. I miss you, baby," I say aloud, closing my eyes as I take a seat. The light breeze feels like a soft caress against my skin in response. As it blows past, it causes small ripples to dance across the lake's surface.

I take a moment to just sit in the calm, and the smell of pine trees wraps around me as the wind continues to blow.

Taking a deep breath, I speak to Sherri, out loud. "I met someone—" I start and then pause, trying to gather my thoughts. "I met her not too long after I lost you, but I didn't start to see her as more than a friend until recently."

I reach my hand into my pocket, pulling out the well-worn envelope. "I carry this letter with me to remind me of the promises I made to you. In our vows . . . in your final week." My voice catches as my emotions get lodged in my throat. "I got promoted to chief—like you knew I would—and the first person, aside from Tessa, that I wanted to share the news with was Gwen, because I knew how happy she would be for me."

Sucking in a deep breath, I look out across the lake and see a family of ducks swimming, the mother duck dipping under the water to cool herself off. "But if I'm being honest with myself, I'm a little overwhelmed with the feelings I have for her. Baby, you were my one and only love—my happily ever after. How will there ever be room in my heart for someone else? She doesn't deserve to be second tier—a replacement—for who I lost." I shake my head.

"Okay, I don't feel like Gwen would be a replacement. But the fear of giving my heart over to someone that isn't you terrifies me." A tear slips from my eye. Reaching up, I wipe it away.

I sit there in silence after revealing my current fears to the empty lake. My gaze slowly moves around the area, taking in the view that Sherri so often came to in order to find peace. Grabbing for my food, I catch sight of a red bird hopping on the corner of the dock. A cardinal—it's black eyes staring at me unblinking.

"Sherri," I whisper, before the bird flies away.

Chapter 24

Gwen

As soon as I step foot out of my office building, my phone vibrates. I smile as I look at it, seeing my twin's picture flash across the screen. "Hey, I'm headed home from work now. Do you want me to stop and get anything on my way?" I ask, answering the phone. My sister, Brandi, is in town for the weekend, which was perfect considering Paul and I hadn't seen much of each other the past few days and she offered to stay with Max so we could spend some time together.

There's a muffled noise on the other end of the phone before Brandi responds. "No, I'm good with raiding your pantry." She chuckles before letting out a sharp gasp. "Unless you don't have food. You do have food, don't you? Wait a minute, do you starve Max? Is that why he called, wanting me to visit? He's not getting proper nutrition?" My eyes roll as my sister continues on.

"Stop lying. Max is not the one who invited you. You invited yourself, you freak. And of course I have food in the pantry. Plenty for you and Max to stuff your faces with." The phone switches to the speaker as I turn on my van.

Brandi's boisterous laugh cuts through the silence. "But really, he's okay with me coming and staying, right? He doesn't feel like I'm overstepping?" she asks, a tinge of something like worry lacing her voice.

Sighing, I find myself rolling my eyes again. "Bran, all he knows is that you're coming to visit because you finally have a weekend off. I didn't tell him that you're planning on probing him with questions about his seizures to help you with work." I don't love that she wants to use my son for her project at work, but I told her she could ask him if he was comfortable answering questions so she can impress her new neurologist boss.

"Does he know that you plan on going out with a certain sexy police widower while I'm there?" she asks, changing the subject.

"Super sexy police *chief* widower." I let out a laugh, matching the one she let out earlier. "And he does know that I'll be going out with Paul, yes. Is he thrilled? No. He still doesn't like the idea of me seeing someone." My heart hammers as my mind silently asks, *Are you ready to be seeing someone?*

The muffled noise sounds from her end of the phone again. "Shoot, that was my exit!" she yells. "Sis, I'll see you in an hour. Love you muchly!"

Before I'm able to respond, the call ends with a *click*.

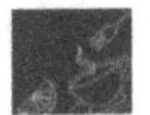

I get home to find Max standing in the kitchen, eating a protein bar. "Hey, Mom."

"Hey, bud. How was school?" I set my purse down and place my keys in a bowl on the counter before walking over to him and kissing him on the forehead.

Max groans while he uses the back of his hand to rub the kiss in. "Mom." He drags out the word and I stifle a chuckle. "It was good. Kyle and I got partnered up on a project for English, so I might have him come over after Aunt Brandi leaves so we can work on it."

Reaching for a bottle of water from the refrigerator, I smile. "That sounds good. I'm sure Brandi wouldn't mind if you invited him over tonight."

He runs his hand through his hair before shaking his head. "Nah. I think it'll be cool to just hang with Aunt Brandi. I haven't seen her in a while." I watch as he walks into the living room and plops down on the couch. "So, you're really going on this date?"

I inhale for a beat, giving myself a chance to collect my thoughts. I knew Max was still unhappy about this, but I thought we'd talked about it. "I am."

"I thought so." He turns on the TV and puts his back to me.

Staring at my reflection in the mirror, Brandi whistles from behind me. I look over my shoulder as she plops herself down on my bed.

"You look hot! Where's he taking you?" she asks, taking a bite of a banana.

I glance at myself again. My wide hips make the burgundy dress flare a little more than it did on the mannequin when I bought it, and my cleavage is on full display as my bra gives my breasts support in the best way. I rotate my curvy hips as I spin—my knee-length dress flowing at the motion—admiring the way my black heels make my calves flex.

"I do, don't I?" I respond with a chuckle. "He's taking me to one of the wineries about thirty minutes out of town. We're taking a cab so neither one of us has to hold back on drinking if we enjoy the wine."

Before I can turn to face my twin, she's standing behind me, her hands messing with my hair. "Let me do your hair. I always love it when it's up. It shows off this gorgeous neck of yours."

Checking the time on my clock, I nod in acceptance. I walk to the dining area to grab a chair, and as I'm heading back, I sneak a peek at Max lying on the living room floor, lost in the game he's playing.

Once I return to my room, I put the chair in front of the mirror and settle down. "Thank you for agreeing to stay with Max while I go on this date," I say to Brandi as she runs the brush through my blonde hair.

She hums before speaking. "Of course. You've been grieving Dwayne alone for long enough. It's time you find someone to make you happy again. Someone to share the sad times with, but also the happy times, too."

Putting the brush down, she picks up her phone. Within seconds, "I Wanna Sex You Up" by Color Me Badd comes through her speaker, causing me to snort.

"Really? This song?" I ask as she grabs the brush again and starts singing.

"You came home and played this song on repeat after you lost your virginity to Toby Scott. It's only fitting I play it before you go off and get laid for the first time by mister sexy police widower—sorry—mister sexy police *chief* widower," Brandi says, pulling my hair into a twisty updo.

My cheeks heat as she talks about me getting laid for the first time by Paul, my mind reminding me *vividly* of our last date. I typically tell my sister everything, but I may have failed to mention what happened *after* we went out before. My silence clues her in on the fact that I'm hiding something because she tugs my hair hard enough to pull my head backward so I'm looking at her upside down.

"Spill."

It's all she has to say; I've never been good at keeping things from her when we're in the same place, or on FaceTime.

"And you better not leave out a single *veiny* detail, you whore."

Rolling my eyes, I let out a breath of defeat. I lean my head forward to see if I can still hear Max's videogame before I turn around to face Brandi. She's taken a seat on the bed again—sitting criss-cross with a pillow in her lap—big blue eyes that match mine staring at me.

As I recount the after-date events, she moves positions to allow herself to kick her feet as she squeals. "Oh my goodness!" she screams, causing me to shush her and poke my head up to listen for signs of my son.

"Okay, so tonight won't be your first time, but from the sounds of it, you very much want it to happen again." Her eyebrows are practically dancing in her hair line while they wiggle up and down.

I shrug my shoulders. "It was . . . incredible. But after, I felt like I was cheating on Dwayne," I admit for the first time. "I know he's gone, but I can't help feeling that way."

She rises to her feet and embraces me in a hug. "Oh, Gwen, that's understandable. You two were together for over twenty years. You said Paul was married to his high school sweetheart, right? I'm sure he felt the same way. Maybe if you talked about it, it might make you feel better. Or is there any other reason for looking like you might puke?" Pulling back from her hug, she eyes me suspiciously while scrunching her nose.

Closing my eyes, I take in a steadying breath. "I'm scared to get close to someone again. To risk falling for someone who could so easily be taken from me." A tear slips from my eye at my admission.

"Oh, Honey." My sister's soft hug embraces me again, wrapping me in the comforting smell of her lavender shampoo. "Your fears are completely valid."

Chapter 25

Paul

The cab pulls into Gwen's driveway about fifteen minutes before I told her I'd be there to pick her up. I sit in the back seat bouncing my knee, debating whether or not to have the driver circle around the neighborhood a time or two so I don't look crazy showing up so early. Before I'm able to say anything, though, the curtain in the front window moves aside and I see Max's face appear.

"I'll only take a few moments," I say to David, the cab driver, as I open the door.

Getting out of the car, I rub my hands down my pants in hopes of calming my nervous energy. I'm wearing khaki pants and a navy blue button-up Tessa said made my eyes pop.

The door opens right as I'm moving to knock, and a woman, who has to be Gwen's sister, stands in front of me. "You must be Paul," she says, leaning in for a hug, "I've heard so much about you." She pulls back and eyes me in an assessing once-over before inviting me in.

"I am. It's nice to meet you. I've heard a lot about you too." I walk in, placing my hands in my pockets and trying to hide the jitters that just started. "Hey, Max, how's it going?" I ask, spotting Gwen's son sitting on the couch, stuffing popcorn in his mouth.

He stares at me unblinking as he chews, making the anxious part of my brain spasm. I've never felt more stressed being around a teenage boy than I do right now.

Brandi—God bless her—must be able to sense the tension because she breaks the silence. "Gwen will be right out. She just needed to finish up with a few things." Her smile widens, showing off two deep dimples, then she walks over to the couch and lightly smacks Max on the arm before grabbing some popcorn from his bowl.

Nodding in acknowledgement, I step closer to the door to wait. Not even a full minute after I turn toward the front window, the air in the room changes. Without turning around I know that Gwen has come out, her vanilla and honey scent wrapping its way around me. I turn slowly, suddenly losing the ability to speak.

She is breathtaking. She's in a burgundy dress that comes right below her knees, with a deep V-neck showing off her cleavage. Her hair is pinned up in a way she hasn't worn around me before and she has a shy smile on her face. I blink a few times while my brain tries to force words to my mouth.

"You look—wow. You look beautiful," I finally say.

A pink tint colors her cheeks as her smile grows. "Thanks. You look good too." She gestures to my outfit, which suddenly feels inadequate. "Okay, I'll be out late tonight. Be good for your aunt and please don't give her a reason to call me. But also, my cell phone will be on in case you *need* to call me. I love you," she says, leaning down and giving Max a kiss on the forehead. Then she leans in to give Brandi a hug and whispers something into her ear, eliciting a giggle from her sister.

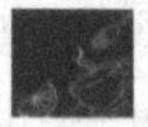

In the cab, David gives us privacy, only speaking when we get back in the car as a greeting. He asks if we want music or if we care if he puts something on for himself. We agree he can have full control over the music as long as it's not so loud we can't hear each other speak.

"Your sister seems nice," I say, trying and failing at finding a topic that doesn't sound lame. *I am fifty-five years old. Why am I being so awkward?*

Gwen smiles and nods. "Yeah, she's pretty great. She's my best friend."

I can tell by the look in her eye that she isn't just say-ing that because they're twins, but because she actually means it. "It must be hard not living closer to her."

Her smile fades slightly before she responds. "It is. But we haven't lived in the same city since we lived at home in high school. She went off to school in Columbus while I stayed closer to home, and then I moved to Lancer with Dwayne after we got married." My heart tightens with unexpected jealousy at the mention of her deceased husband.

"I know you have a sister . . . do you get along well?" she asks, eyes never leaving mine.

I nod my head. "We do. Her family and mine have gone on vacations together every summer since we both started families of our own. Our parents come as well. This summer will be one of the few times I won't be going since it's planned too close to Tessa's due date and I want to be around in case she needs me." My mind thinks of summers past as I talk about some of our previous vacations.

Before I know it, the cab is pulling into the winery parking lot, putting a hold on our conversation. I open my door and quickly run around to open the door for Gwen before she gets a chance to. She takes a few steps away from the car as I lean down to tip David and thank him for getting us here safely.

Grabbing Gwen's hand, I lead us to the front door of the building. I made a reservation for a tasting, which allows us to sit out on the back patio overlooking the vineyard. Walking into the rustic estate, a strong scent of fermented fruit wafts into my nostrils while a soft instrumental version of "Beautiful Things" dances through my ears.

"Good evening, Laura," I say to the hostess. "I have a reservation for Paul Gunter."

She smiles at me and checks the list in front of her on the podium. "Yes. Paul, party of two, reservations for a patio tasting?"

"That's us." I squeeze Gwen's hand slightly.

"Perfect." She grabs two menus and hands them to a waitress who just walked up. "Valerie will take you to your table, if you just follow her."

Chapter 26

Gwen

As we make our way to the back patio, my gaze catches on the view. The restaurant portion of the winery sits atop a hill that looks out over rows and rows of grapevines. Not too far in the distance you can see the outline of the Blue Ridge Mountains. I'm so lost in the scenery that I almost don't realize when Valerie stops walking, indicating that we've reached our table.

"This view is stunning," I say to no one in particular.

While pulling my chair out, Paul responds to my comment. "I hoped you'd like it."

Valerie smiles as she sets the menus down in front of us. "Like Laura said, I'm Valerie. I will be your waitress this evening. Please take your time looking through the menus here . . ." Reaching across the table, she continues. "And we have the wine menu right here. I'll be back shortly to take your order."

I close my eyes, taking a deep breath and inhaling the fresh air as the cool breeze brushes against my face. "I've never been to a winery before," I admit, opening up my menu. "Is it like a regular restaurant with your typical food options, or do they have specific foods that go with certain wines?" I scan the menu before lifting my gaze to lock onto Paul's stare.

"They have both. If you'd like, we can ask Valerie for the special—that dish typically comes with a wine prepared on-site. Or you can order something else and choose any drink that sounds appealing to you." His eyes never leave mine. "Please don't feel like you have to drink wine just because we're at a winery. I want you to have whatever you'd like."

The smile that has become a permanent fixture on my face in his presence grows, causing my cheeks to ache. "Okay, well, what would you recommend?" I ask, placing the menu down.

His eyebrow quirks up slightly and the grin he's wearing causes the smile lines on his sun-kissed face to deepen. He runs a hand through the dusting of facial hair splattered across his cheeks. "I was thinking about getting the special of the day, paired with the recommended wine, but I also thought about asking for a wine flight of the most popular wines they sell."

"That sounds perfect to me." Nodding my head briefly, I move my menu to the side as Valerie walks back up to the table.

Her vibrant red hair bounces in her ponytail as she moves her head to give us both her attention while she speaks. "Have you decided what you'd like to start off with?" she asks, setting down two glasses of ice water.

Paul gives her the details of our order before he turns back to look at me. "Did I forget anything?"

"No, that all sounds great!" I smile at him and look at her as she writes down the last of our order.

"I'll be right out with your wine flight, and the wine that comes with the main course will be delivered with the meal." She grabs the menus from the table before walking away to put the order in.

When it's just the two of us again, my nerves return with the butterflies that seem to have taken up residence in my stomach. His bright blue eyes watch me carefully, causing flashbacks of when our eyes locked while I strad-dled him on his bed to flit through my mind. I feel my face heat up at the memory and then guilt washes over me, dousing the fire that was trying to ignite in my core as I recall my conversation with Brandi.

Seemingly aware of the shift in my mind, Paul's gaze turns concerned. "What's wrong?"

My eyes sting with tears wanting to break free. I shake my head, trying to dislodge the feeling that I'm betraying Dwayne. *Talk to him. Be honest.*

"I told you on our first maybe-date that I'm too old for games and that I believe in honesty. So, I need to tell you something." Taking a slow breath, I watch his eyes, but he doesn't waver, he just nods to acknowledge I've got his attention. "I've enjoyed our time together, starting with our first encounter with the group, to us sitting on your truck in my driveway. But I feel like I'm cheating. My brain knows Dwayne is gone, but in my heart, it feels like I'm doing something wrong." I look down at my lap, my fingers twisting together.

Risking a look, I see his expression has turned from one of concern to one of understanding and my heart slows from its accelerated nervous pounding. "Gwen, I get it. Honestly, I've been struggling because I feel the same way. When you left my house after our putt-putt date I was racked with guilt."

It's then that Valerie brings our wine samples to the table. She explains each one and asks if we'd like her to go through the flavors of each as we try them or if we want to drink them at our leisure. We both agree that she doesn't need to stay at our table, but we thank her for offering.

Once she leaves, Paul picks up where he left off. "I don't want you to get the wrong idea. I don't regret a single thing that's happened between us, but while lying in bed—in the house and room I shared my whole adult life with Sherri—I feel that same pang of guilt. That I'm not being faithful to her." He reaches his hand out across the table, palm up, silently asking for my hand. I tentatively place mine atop his.

"But there's also a difference between my situation and yours, and I recognize that too. I was aware I was going to lose Sherri—we had a chance to say our goodbyes. And no matter how hard it was, she was able to share her wishes that I find someone new. You lost Dwayne in such a fast and unexpected way. Yes, it's been a few years, but it's understandable *if* you haven't fully accepted that you can find someone new too." His thumb draws a lazy design on the back of my hand as the words sink in.

Tears softly fall from my eyes as I look at Paul—really look at him. The truth and wisdom in what he said—the weight of it—sits on my shoulders, but it doesn't feel heavy. It feels as though I'm finally able to take a deep breath for the first time in two years.

Chapter 27

Paul

Once we've talked about our mutual feelings of guilt over this new relationship we're navigating, the evening becomes more relaxed. Our dinner—roasted chicken and vegetables paired with a crisp white wine—is filled with easy conversation where we take turns sharing stories of our day-to-day life. I can't help but notice how talking to her about the ins and outs of life feels so natural.

"What's a secret about you that nobody knows?" Gwen changes the conversation while sticking her fork through a piece of broccoli.

Leaning back in my chair, I fix my gaze out on the view. "Something nobody knows . . . Hmm." I rub my hand over my stubble as I genuinely think about my answer. "I'm afraid of clowns." She lets out a laugh that causes my heart to leap.

"You're afraid of clowns? I find it hard to believe you've gone fifty-five years with nobody finding that out." She looks at me pointedly.

Nodding my head at her confusion, I say, "I can see where you'd think that. But Sherri loved clowns. Actually, both her and Tessa loved going to the circus, and they always wanted to get pictures with the clowns after. My hands would shake and my shirt would be soaked with sweat after because of my fear, but every year, I took them to the circus because it made my girls happy." I shudder at the memory of white faces with creepy smiles painted over their mouths and their oversized shoes.

Her laughing has stopped and she's sitting there with her chin resting in her palms as her elbows are propped on the table. The smile on her face is hard to read, but no less beautiful than every other smile she's ever blessed me with.

"What?" I ask as she continues to stare at me.

Shaking her head, she picks her head up, her eyes shining brightly as she talks. "I always knew you were a good one. But listening to the fact that—year after year—you put yourself through clown hell because your wife and daughter loved it? That's just more proof."

A sense of pride sparks through me at the compliment. I never did fun things for my family so people would think I was a good person. I did it because seeing the happiness on their faces was reward enough for me. Those pictures, even though there are scary clowns in them, still bring joy to my heart because they carry the memories with them.

I notice a blush spread across Gwen's cheeks seconds before she says, "Are you ready to get out of here? Maybe we can go back to your place for a bit?"

Suddenly, I forget how to speak and my throat goes dry. Picking up my wine glass, I nod my head. I wave to the waitress, ask for the bill, and pull up the app for a ride share to pick us up. All the while, Gwen is watching me with a look on her face that has my cock stiffening beneath my pants.

On the ride back to my place, I feel a calmness settle over my body. My hand rests on her thigh and her finger rubs along the back of it, lazily, as she talks. "Max has been dying to do one of those escape rooms, so I think we might try to do one while Brandi's in town."

"I haven't done one before, but I've heard they're fun," I say, thinking about one of the ladies at work talking about how she went to one for a girls' night.

"Brandi enjoys getting out of the house when we're together, so she's definitely taking advantage of Max wanting to do this."

My thumb grazes against her dress, her voice animated while she talks about her sister.

The conversation comes to a stop as the cab pulls up to my house. I grab my wallet out of my pocket to reach for cash as Gwen gets out of the car. By the time I've finished tipping and make my way to the porch, she has her cell phone in her hand and is resting with her hip against the railing.

Her lip lifts up in a slow smile before her tongue slowly slides out of her mouth and rubs against her lips. "Brandi texted and said Max couldn't hang—he fell asleep already. So there's no rush to get me home before curfew." She chuckles.

My eyes shamelessly glide down her figure. "How about we head inside then?" My voice is huskier than usual.

Her pupils dilate as she sucks in a breath. Swallowing, she bites her bottom lip and nods. Stepping up to the door, I unlock it and push it open, moving to the side so Gwen can walk past me.

Unlike the last time Gwen entered my home, she's taking in the scenery. She slowly looks at the pictures hanging on the wall in the foyer—Tessa throughout the years, with a few family photos scattered in between.

She stops at one and leans in close to study it. Her eyelashes flicker, eyes bouncing around the image. It's a picture of Sherri, Tessa, and I when we went to Tennessee one summer. Tessa is a carbon copy of Sherri in their matching yellow dresses and their long, curly, golden brown hair cascading down the front of their shoulders. The girls are smiling at the camera while my gaze is fixed on Sherri.

"She was really beautiful," Gwen says, standing back up to her full height.

My eyes are transfixed on Gwen. "Yes, she was." Smiling, I observe her as she walks the rest of the way into the house.

I feel a tightening in my chest as I take in this gorgeous woman in the house I lived in with Sherri my whole adult life. The guilt tries to grip my heart, but then I think back to our conversation at dinner, and the letter sitting on my nightstand—the reminder that Sherri wanted me to move on. She wanted me to find happiness. Once that realization kicks in, I make my way over to Gwen. Spinning her around to face me, I grip her neck and pull her into a kiss.

Chapter 28

Gwen

Taking a small step forward, I press my body into Paul, trying to deepen the kiss—needing to be closer to him. The smell of pine and lemon wraps me in a hug as I fight to mirror his pace. The desire to take his clothes off grows stronger as his hands firmly hold onto my neck.

Before I can still myself, my hands are reaching up and unbuttoning his shirt. He loosens his grip and I let out a small whimper in disappointment. One of his hands trails the length of my arm, meeting my hands at his buttons and he pulls up, untucking his shirt, sliding his arm out of the sleeve. He removes his other hand from me, making goose bumps pimple across my skin at the loss of contact, so he can fully remove his top.

The whole time our mouths remain locked in a frenzied kiss. Paul slowly pulls back to lift off his undershirt, leaving him bare-chested in front of me. I gulp while I unabashedly check him out. Reaching my hand up, I run my fingers through the smattering of graying curly chest hair that covers him.

His hand moves to the zipper at the side of my dress, eyes searching mine for any hesitation. Reaching up, I take over, pulling the zipper down and shrugging the dress off my shoulders. My body warms from the heat radiating from him while he takes in the matching lace undergarments I'm wearing.

"Bedroom?" he asks, taking a finger and running it down the front of my bra. My nipples pebble at the movement.

I nod before my brain can form a sentence, then add, "If that's where you want to go." I glance around the room. It's been a while since I've had sex anywhere but a bed, but I'm seriously contemplating pulling him to the couch.

"Or . . ." He loops his pointer finger around my bra strap, causing it to slide down my shoulder. "We could stay here." He leans down, placing a gentle kiss on the indent the strap left.

"Here's good," I whisper, my head lolling back while he trails kisses down the lace fabric covering my breasts.

He guides me back to the couch, lips and tongue tracing the edge of my bra the entire time. As soon as my legs meet the sofa, I reach behind me and unclasp my bra, needing to free myself. Once it slides down my arms, I toss it aside and sit down. Biting my lip, I trail my finger down his happy trail to the buckle on his belt.

Making quick work of his belt and button I look up at Paul through my lashes. "Is this okay?" I ask, grazing the top of his pants.

"Definitely." It comes out a whisper.

The moment I get the go-ahead, I rid him of his pants and boxer briefs at the same time, his erection standing at attention. A shiny droplet of pre-cum rests at the tip of his cock. Without a second thought, I grip him around his shaft and wrap my mouth around the head.

Paul's hands fly to my head, gently tugging at my hair, a moan flying out of his mouth. "Fuck! That feels—*fuck*."

Stifling a laugh at his response, I take him deeper into my mouth. His cock hits my throat, making me gag slightly, causing him to pull back. Stopping him with my hands on his ass—repositioning myself—I take in a deep breath through my nose and bring him as far back as I can. Swallowing around his cock is a bit difficult, but it pulls him deeper and the sound that leaves his body is worth the brief discomfort.

With my hands still placed on his ass, I encourage him to thrust his hips. "Are you sure?" he asks, his voice husky.

I nod my head and dig my nails into his rear. The sting that causes must ignite a flame within him because he starts thrusting with purpose. While he's got my hair in his grip, I move one hand from his backside to cup his balls. They tighten at the sudden attention.

"Gwen—I'm close."

I pull back and squeeze my tits together. "Come here."

With that simple command, he finds his release all over my chest. As the warm sticky cum slides down over my nipples, I instantly feel a wetness pool in my panties.

Chapter 29

Paul

Watching my cum cover Gwen's tits is probably the sexiest thing I've seen in a long time. She takes a finger and drags it along my release, bringing it to her mouth . . . and sucks.

"Fuck," I groan. I take back my earlier thought—*that's* the sexiest thing I've seen in a long time.

Even though I just came, I can feel myself slowly harden again. "Let's go clean you up." I bend down, picking her up bridal style.

I walk with her in my arms until we reach my en suite. Carefully placing her down, I stick my arm in the shower to turn on the water. She watches me with blue eyes full of lust, her gorgeous blonde hair in a tangle from where I was gripping her while I fucked her mouth.

We stand there, just watching each other, while the room fills with steam. Reaching my arm back in the shower to check the temperature, I nod at her, my dick already standing at attention again. She removes her panties at a glacial pace, teasing me.

"Like what you see, big guy?"

I nod. Instinctively reaching toward her, I bite my lower lip. She takes me by my left hand and guides it down to her pussy. My finger glides between her slick lips—drenched from how wet she is. *Fuck.*

"Holy fuck, Gwen. You're soaked." I growl. I never growl.

A whimper leaves her mouth, but she continues to control my hand at her entrance. Her slender fingers wrap around mine, and ever so slowly, she pushes my index and middle fingers inside herself.

I watch, transfixed, as she uses me. Her other hand traces up her body and she tweaks her peaked nipple with her thumb and forefinger. Needing to do something, I reach my right hand to her other nipple. The additional pressure causes a breathy moan to leave her.

"Yes . . ." she sighs. "You can pinch a little harder," Gwen encourages.

Taking a step closer to her, the hand at her pussy tilts to a different angle and I take this opportunity to adjust myself, moving my thumb to put pressure on her clit. I lean down and take her pebbled nipple into my mouth, her skin salty from her sweat and what's leftover from me.

I feel her body move, her head leaning back. "Fucking hell. You really know what you're doing," she praises, her hand abandoning mine, allowing me to take over.

I guide her backward so she's resting against my counter. My tongue twirls around her nipple and my fingers curl inside her pulsing pussy. Slowly, I move my mouth down her body, kissing, nipping, and licking my way to meet my hand. I stop at the scar she was so insecure about during our first time, placing a kiss on it before continuing my way to her pussy.

When my mouth reaches its destination, I remove my thumb and take over with my tongue. I swirl it around her clit, all the while my fingers continue the same rhythm. Gwen's hand finds my head—with no hair to hold on to—and she puts slight pressure on my scalp with her fingernails, the feeling sends a shiver through my body.

Her breathing becomes erratic as her walls start to clamp around my fingers. I feel her body tense as she struggles to stay upright but also fights to let herself ride the wave of her orgasm. Wrapping my arm around the back of her to give more support, I continue sucking and nipping at her clit.

I'm about to switch up my technique since she hasn't said anything, but then I taste her, and she's coming all over my fingers and mouth. It's the most glorious flavor I've ever tasted—the perfect mix between salty and sweet.

I gently lick her pussy as cum continues to leak out of her and shift my gaze to her face. She's wearing a sated smile, her eyes glossy and her body flushed. The definition of beautiful.

Standing up, I lean down and wrap her in a hug, and she angles her head so she can give me a quick kiss. "Are you ready to get in the shower, now that it's probably turned cold?" I laugh into her hair.

"Hmm. A cold shower would probably do us both a bit of good." She giggles.

I wake up and look at the clock—two a.m. Rubbing my eyes, I glance next to me and see Gwen sound asleep. We didn't plan for her to spend the night, but after the shower we decided to cuddle in bed and watch a movie. She fell asleep twenty minutes in and I didn't have the heart to wake her up.

Carefully removing myself from bed, I get up to go to the bathroom. When I return, I watch her for a few moments—her golden blonde hair sprawled on my pillow, arm tucked under her head, her mouth slightly open as she breathes. It hits me at that moment.

I think I'm falling in love, and it doesn't scare me as much as I used to think it would.

When I climb back into bed, Gwen scoots closer to me, as if we're two magnets being pulled together by our poles. I burrow down in the covers a bit more and she moves her head to my chest without even opening her eyes. My whole body relaxes as I wrap my arm around her, like the most natural thing in the world.

Chapter 30

Gwen

Opening my front door and tiptoeing in quietly has me feeling like a teenager again. Flashes of sneaking home way past curfew run through my mind, causing a giggle to erupt from my throat. Once the door's shut behind me, I finally look ahead of me and see Max sitting at the table, a spoonful of cereal halfway to his mouth.

Shit. My seventeen-year-old son just caught me doing the walk of shame. "Hey, Bud." I straighten my back and tug at the straps on my dress.

His eyebrows are practically in his hairline as he sits, observing me. "Hey, Aunt Brandi . . . How long ago did my mom hop in the shower?" Max yells across the house.

I take this time to walk toward the kitchen, forcing my head to stay high. *I did nothing wrong.*

"She hopped in about ten minutes ago. Why—" Brandi stops dead in her tracks, her eyes catching sight of me at the coffee pot, pouring myself a mug.

Max looks at me again, a smug smile creeping across his face. "Were you out all night, Mother?"

Heat creeps up my chest and settles on my cheeks under the scrutiny from both my teenager and my sister. I can either lie to him—which would be pointless since I'm wearing the dress from last night—or I can be honest.

Taking a deep breath, I nod my head. "I was. After dinner we went back to his place to watch a movie. I fell asleep during it, and like the gentleman he is, he let me sleep." There, the truth isn't so bad.

A snort leaves Brandi. She walks up and leans on the counter next to me, arching an eyebrow. "A movie? You think he believes that?" she whispers to me, but my eyes don't leave Max. He wasn't fond of the idea of me going on this date, so I need to see his reaction.

He looks at me for a beat longer, eyes narrowing before he returns to his bowl of cereal. Letting out a deep sigh, I relax my shoulders.

"I guess I can go turn the shower off now," Brandi says from beside me, causing a laugh to break free.

"I don't see why we had to invite them," Max grumbles, climbing out of the back seat of the van.

Brandi answers before I get a chance. "Because I'd like to know the guy taking my sister out and letting her crash on his *couch*."

"And you like Tessa and Graham, so I thought it'd be nice to invite them along too. Plus, the more people involved in an escape room, the quicker we can get out," I say, pulling him into a side hug.

Before Brandi arrived, Max mentioned wanting to go to an escape room as one of the activities while she was in town. One mention of Paul and she quickly said he had to be invited too. I thought asking his daughter and her husband along would help Max feel less uncomfortable. But watching Paul, Graham, and Tessa get out of their car, I can't help but hope I wasn't wrong.

"I hope you guys like Clue!" Brandi says loudly as our group walks to the door. "This place has special themed rooms that switch every month. This month is Clue, so I booked it for us!"

A wicked smile spreads across Tessa's face while Graham and Paul look at each other with wide eyes.

"That feels ominous," I mumble in Max's ear, causing a chuckle.

Once we've checked in, we're led to a very large room where each of us pick an item that represents the characters from the game, and are handed an envelope. Inside the envelopes, is information that lets us know our role at the party. Five of the envelopes have a single word—guest. The final envelope has three words written in it—murderer, a weapon, and a room.

"Welcome to Clue!" the young employee says with a smile on his face. "You were all invited to dinner, only to arrive and find the host has been murdered. The goal of this escape room is to find clues that will allow you to discover who the murderer is. But there's a twist . . ." He gives a brief pause to look at each of us. "You were all given an envelope, which are only for your eyes, because within those envelopes you will find that one of you is the murderer. Your goal as the murderer is to try to thwart any progress being made at finding you out. You all have sixty-five minutes, which start the moment I walk back out the door. Do you have any questions?"

We all look at each other before shaking our heads, all in agreement we don't have any. The young man nods his head once, says, "Good luck," and turns to walk out the door as we all stand there, assessing one another. My card says guest, so my goal is to figure out who in the group I can trust.

I look around the room and see it's set up into nine smaller sections, each one representing a room from the game. I walk over to the closest one and pick up a book. "This must be the Library," I say to the group, holding the book that clearly says *LIBRARY* across it.

"Y'all, look here, I'm going to the Conservatory," Max says, walking across the room. The group exchanges glances. *Why would Max want to look at a different room if he wasn't the murderer?*

"That's a good idea. I think we should all split up and look for clues within the other rooms and meet back at the Hall in, say . . . twenty minutes, to go over what we've found," Tessa says. *Maybe she's the murderer.*

I watch as the members of our group slowly walk to different sections of the room. Fuck. This is going to be tougher than I thought.

"Do you have any thoughts so far?" Paul asks from behind me, causing me to jump. "Oops, sorry. I should've made a noise or something."

"Well, the game just started. But . . . Max threw me off by saying he was going to look in the Conservatory. But then Tessa agreed we should split up. So, I'm not sure."

Nodding, he looks around the room. "We have to be careful of Tessa. This is her favorite board game. If she isn't just a guest, it'll be hard to tell." My eyes scan the room until I catch sight of her. She's sitting on a couch rubbing her belly as she looks over a piece of paper in, what I'm assuming is, the Lounge.

"I found something!" Graham calls from the Kitchen. Our heads jerk in his direction.

"Babe! We agreed we'd bring our findings to the Hall." Tessa huffs.

I watch as Graham's cheeks pinken. "Shit, you're right. Carry on!" Paul and I laugh from our position still in the Library.

Chapter 31

Paul

Checking the clock on the wall that tells us how much time we have left, I notice it's nearing the twenty-minute mark. "I guess I should go look for clues of my own before Tessa gets angry that I didn't contribute." I chuckle before walking away from Gwen, heading to the section set-up as the Ballroom.

I look at the walls and notice a picture of the characters from the game. All of the characters are faded in coloring, except one. I make a note of it before looking around the room at each person in their character garb. Gwen as Mrs. White, Brandi as Miss Scarlett, Tessa as Mrs. Peacock, Max as Mr. Green, Graham as Professor Plum, and myself as Colonel Mustard.

Tessa is waddling her way over to the Hall and I take one final look around the Ballroom. I notice a scarf dangling from the side of the piano and a picture of Miss Scarlett sitting right next to it.

"Okay, guys, it's been twenty minutes! Back to the Hall to put our clues together to see if we need to keep looking!" Tessa's voice is loud, even in the large space.

"I found purple cards in the Conservatory, and purple means Professor Plum. So maybe he did it?" Max says, holding up a deck of purple playing cards.

Brandi nods her head in what looks like agreement. "I found a picture of a purple wrench in the dining room. Maybe Professor Plum did it with the Wrench in the Conservatory."

Tessa rolls her eyes, clearly not convinced. "Okay, but the color purple doesn't mean it's Professor Plum. In the Lounge, I saw a bunch of colored objects that could represent any number of us." She looks at everyone suspiciously. "Babe, what did you find in the Kitchen?"

He holds up a picture of Miss Scarlett holding a knife in front of a cooked turkey. "I think this makes it look like Miss Scarlett could've done it with the Knife. There's photographic evidence of her *holding* the potential weapon."

Brandi lets out a *humph* sound.

"Dad, Gwen, did you find anything?" Tessa looks between the two of us.

I tip my chin to Gwen, signalling she can go first. "I found a plastic revolver stuffed behind a book on one of the shelves. Maybe whoever it was did it with the Revolver. I don't think it was done in the Library, though. It was too obvious of a hiding spot if that was the case."

Everyone looks at me for my clues. "I saw a rope hanging off the edge of the piano in the Ballroom." Wincing, I look at Brandi before saying the next part. "There was a framed picture of Miss Scarlett next to it."

"I didn't do it!" Brandi practically yells. "I think we should take a few more minutes to look for more clues.

I don't think we have enough to make a proper guess. I, for one, would like to find more evidence that it was Professor Plum." She doesn't give anyone a chance to argue before she turns around and heads to the Billiard Room.

Gwen giggles from next to me. The sound is a melody I would love to make the soundtrack for my life. "She's taking this so seriously."

I trail behind Max to the Dining Room. "Do you want any help?"

He turns his head and stares at me. "No, I think I'm good. I was headed to the Study."

I glance back from the direction we were just in. "Isn't the Study on the other side of the Hall?"

Nodding his head once, he walks back toward the Study. *Well, that went well.*

Ten more minutes pass, and we've reconvened in the Hall. "Okay, I know it's only been thirty-five minutes since we started and, we technically have thirty minutes left . . . But I'd really like to finish ahead of schedule. What new clues have we found?" Tessa sits on one of the chairs in the small section.

"I found a picture of Colonel Mustard and the host in the Study. It looked like a hunting picture, so that's proof that they were together with guns," Max says, eyeing me as if *I* was the suspect.

Gwen smiles at her son and adds, "I saw a newspaper article on the desk in the Study that had the word 'candlestick' in bold. The image with it was of Mrs. White."

"Hon, I don't think you're supposed to give clues that make it look like *you* did it," Brandi whispers loud enough for everyone to hear.

Gwen shrugs her shoulders. "If I'm the killer I'm doing a bad job at thwarting guesses since I'm offering up clues that point to me."

Everyone tosses out a few more clues while Tessa scribbles some notes on a piece of paper, her eyes flicking between the words she has written and everyone standing around. "I think I know, but I want to walk around each room one more time. I'll come up to everyone and share what I have written and explain my thoughts to see if everyone agrees. If we all agree then we can make the announcement to see if we win."

"Tess, I love you, but why do *you* get to be in charge? What if it's Mrs. Peacock and you're using all this to outwit us?" Graham asks the question I'm sure everyone was thinking.

I know I was.

Tessa glares at him. "I've only written down what clues everyone has said. If anyone thinks I'm missing something then they can say so when I talk to them." She storms off toward the Ballroom.

Standing in the Hall, looking for any clues that may have been missed, I spot Tessa talking with Gwen. They're looking over the notes and whispering. Seeing my two girls get along tugs at my heart, making a smile spread across my face.

After a few moments I hear, "Hey, Dad," as Tessa comes up behind me.

I look at the sheet of paper in her hand and smile. "Hey, Bug. My turn to go over the notes with you?"

As soon as the words leave my mouth, the rest of the group walks into the Hall. "We'd like to make our guess now," Gwen says loudly so the employee can hear her over the speaker.

Tilting my head in confusion, my eyebrows crease. "But I didn't get a chance to go over the notes," I say to Tessa.

"Go ahead. What's your guess?" The employee's voice breaks through the room.

Gwen nods at Tessa, who peers at everyone else who all shake their heads in mutual agreement. "The murderer is Colonel Mustard, with the Revolver, in the Ballroom," Tessa says without hesitation.

The employee clicks on the speaker again. "Does everyone agree before I lock that in as your final guess?"

An echo of yeses sound from around me, and I just stand there slack-jawed. Waiting for the worker to say whether their guess was correct, I reach my hand into my back pocket, pulling out my envelope. Opening it and peeking at the slip of paper, I let out a soft laugh.

"That is . . . correct. Congratulations for completing the escape room in forty-six minutes. That's a new record here at Locked-In." Once he's done speaking, the room erupts with applause . . . including my own.

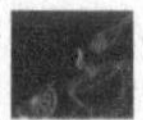

"What was the final clue that gave me away?" I ask, sitting down at Gwen's table. She invited us all back to her place for pizza after we finished the escape room.

Tessa and Gwen share a look before Gwen says, "For one, you spent a lot of time in the Ballroom but never mentioned the picture—the one where all the characters *but* Colonel Mustard were faded."

"For another, when you were blaming *me*, you said there was a *rope* hanging off the piano. It was a *scarf*. That was plain rude," Brandi pipes in.

I bark out a laugh. "I should never have doubted Tessa would figure it out. She's got an eye for details."

Tess shakes her head. "It was actually Max who saw it was a scarf and not a rope." She tips her chin at him before taking a bite of her pizza.

Smiling at Max, I take a bite of the crust in my hand. "Nice work, Bud."

Max tosses his slice onto his plate. "You know what, you don't need to be so nice to me. You don't need to pretend to be my dad or something. My dad is dead! I killed him!" He stands up and runs to his room.

Gwen excuses herself and chases after Max and my jaw tightens, trying not to let my mouth gape open. Looking around the table, I see everyone else has lost the battle of schooling their own faces.

Chapter 32

Gwen

Cautiously, I sit at the foot of Max's bed while he lies face down on his pillow. I hesitantly ask, "Do you want to talk about that outburst now, or in the morning?"

He doesn't answer at first, just wiggles his legs. I hear the conversation resume at the table, Brandi's laughter filling the quiet of Max's bedroom.

"We can talk about it now." He rolls over and sits up so his back is against the headboard.

I wait patiently, letting him guide the conversation. His gaze is on his hands, watching his fingers fiddle with the hem of his shirt. A reluctant sigh leaves him, then he says, "I miss Dad." He blinks a few times before looking up at me. "I was having fun tonight, but then it felt too real. Paul is *not* my dad, and the realization of that made me feel mad . . . and guilty. *I'm* the reason he isn't here anymore."

A tear slides down my cheek at the sound of his voice breaking.

Standing up, I walk to the head of his bed and climb in next to him. "Oh, Baby, we talked about this. It wasn't your fault. There was no way to know that you would have a seizure when driving—you'd never had one be-fore." I pull him into me and he rests his head on my shoulder.

"That might be true, but I'm still the reason he isn't here. Even if it was an accident, I'm the reason we won't be able to discover Dad is the murderer in an escape room. Dad can never compliment me and tell me I did a good job again. And even if it wasn't something we could have planned for, it *is* my fault." Max hiccups and tears start falling from his eyes.

Running through the emergency room doors, I head straight to the nurses' desk. "Max—Maxwell Waters! Where is he? That's my son!" How I made it to the hospital without causing a crash of my own is a miracle.

The nurse starts typing on her keyboard seconds before a man speaks behind me. "Mrs. Waters?" Turning, I see a cop standing there with a look of sympathy etched across his otherwise flawless face.

"Yes, that's me," I whimper.

"Ma'am, I'm Officer Decker. We spoke on the phone." I nod in recognition of the name. "You can follow me. Your son is this way."

We turn down a long hallway, and the strong smell of antiseptics and disinfectant hits my nose. Passing by rooms with closed doors and hushed voices, my eyes roam the nurses station, as if I can tell just by sight which staff mem-bers are assigned to work on my son.

"He's right in here, ma'am. I'll let you go in and see him, but then I have a few questions for you," Officer Decker says, holding open the door to room eleven.

I take a deep breath before I step in, the scent of rubbing alcohol an assault on my senses. As soon as I walk through the door, I see Max, attached to an IV, cuts and bruises covering his face and left arm, a white gauzy bandage above his left eye, and his right arm in a blue cast resting atop his stomach. His chest rises and falls, breaths shallow. Sleeping. Alive.

Grabbing his left hand, I sit in the chair beside his bed and start crying . . . again. "Oh, Baby, I'm so sorry this happened." My thumb rubs along the backside of his hand.

About five minutes pass before we're joined by a doctor. "Hello, you must be Mrs. Waters. I'm Doctor Castro, and I'm the head physician in charge of Maxwell's case." She reaches her hand out to shake mine.

"I'm going to just go through all we know right now, though we still have tests we'd like to run. But I imagine, as a parent, your mind is probably focused on what we know at the moment." Doctor Castro pauses before looking at her tablet. "Maxwell was brought in via ambulance from the scene of a car accident. He arrived unconscious, but has since woken up. He had abrasions on his face and arms—the abrasion above his left eye was deep enough to need sutures. His left arm had a transverse fracture resulting in the need for a cast."

She takes a moment to let the information she just gave settle in. I give a brief nod encouraging her to continue, not brave enough to use my voice. "He went in for a CT scan *when he first arrived and, other than the superficial injuries, nothing was found—"*

Her briefing is cut off by Max gasping for air, followed by his body convulsing. She immediately runs to Max's side and presses a button on the bed signaling for more help to come. Backing up to give space to the nurses rushing into the room, I bump into the wall, nearly collapsing to the floor in the process.

I rub Max's back while he lies down, slowly drifting to sleep. "It's not your fault, Baby. I wish you could understand that."

Once his breathing evens out, I pull the covers over him and place a kiss on his forehead. Walking to his door, I turn back one last time to watch him sleep before joining everyone back in the dining room.

Opening my eyes, I strain my ears, trying to focus on the sound that woke me up. Is that . . . singing? Sitting up in bed, I look at the clock and see it's almost eight in the morning.

I actually slept in.

I climb out of bed, wrap myself in my gray robe, and trod out to the kitchen. A smile spreads across my face with the sight of Brandi and Max cooking together and singing "My Girl." That was Dwayne's favorite song. He would sing it to me at all hours of the day. And when Max was old enough to sing, he'd join in.

Leaning against the doorframe, I watch the two of them dance around the kitchen. It's a welcome sight after Max's breakdown last night. It's been a long time since I've seen him truly smile and laugh the way he is right now. An ache fills my heart as I think about his words last night.

I'm the reason he's not here anymore.

Before the memory pulls me under, Max catches sight of me and points at me while singing the chorus. A wet-sounding laugh escapes me, and I fight back tears threatening to fall. Dancing my way to the kitchen to join my sister and son, I sing along as the song finishes.

"Thank you," I say to Brandi while we clean up the kitchen after breakfast.

"For what?"

I stop scrubbing the pan used for pancakes to look at her. "The shift in his attitude this morning. Singing with him, making him laugh." I glance over the island at Max, lying on his stomach playing some game.

She shakes her head before responding. "No need to thank me. He was actually singing in here when I woke up. I just decided to join him instead of giving him shit for being tone-deaf."

Leaning against the counter, pan forgotten in the sink, I stare at Max with a smile on my face. *He's going to be okay.*

Brandi bumps her hip against mine, and giving me a shit-eating grin, she says, "So . . . Now that I've seen how good-looking Paul is, give me the tea. How big is his dick? Is he good in bed? No, you know what? Forget that last question. You *spent the night!* Of course he's good in bed. If he wasn't, you would've dipped."

I let out a loud cackle at her questioning. I should've prepared myself for this, but when she didn't ask for details while we were getting ready for the escape room, I thought I was in the clear. I really should've known better.

Without saying a word, I hold my hands up, gesturing an absurd size. Brandi's eyes bug out of her face. "Shut the fuck up! You go girl!"

"Get out of here! I'm not fifteen anymore; I'm not going to spill the details of my sex life." I push at her shoulder, an exasperated sigh leaving her.

"You used to be fun. You told me how big Dwayne was. Why can't I know how big Paul is? Is he bigger, or smaller?" She bounces her eyebrows. "Just use your fingers to tell me. I won't tell anyone." When she realizes I'm not going to tell her, she huffs out a breath before sticking her tongue out and shouting, "Boo!"

I finish cleaning up the kitchen and join Brandi and Max in the living room to enjoy the last few hours we get with my sister.

Chapter 33

Gwen

It's been a month since Brandi came to visit and Max blew up at dinner. During that time, Tessa and Graham have opened their home to us for their weekly game nights with Paul. Max seems to enjoy himself, and hasn't had any more outbursts, but he stays quiet most of the time. He has, however, gone to their house alone a few times, allowing Paul and I have time to ourselves.

Today I have a lunch date with Paul, but he's still not here. After twenty minutes of waiting with no texts and unanswered phone calls, my anxiety and fear start to kick in.

Taking a deep breath, I dial the number to the police station, silently praying he's in a meeting and forgot to call.

"Hello, Middleburg Police Department, this is Faith. How may I direct your call?" The woman's friendly voice slightly puts me at ease.

Luckily, I've met Faith a few times, so I don't feel as foolish when I speak. "Hi, Faith, this is Gwen . . . Waters. Is Chief Gunter in?"

A silence stretches on her side, making my anxiety rage again. "Gwen, hey. No, Chief Gunter isn't in right now, there was an accident—"

My mind shuts off entirely, and I stop registering my surroundings. My hands tremble so badly I drop my phone before I hear the rest. If I weren't already sitting down, I'm positive my legs would have collapsed. *This can't be happening . . . again.*

Chapter 34

Paul

Pulling up to the car accident, I realize I left my phone on my desk so I can't call or text Gwen to let her know I'll be late for lunch. As chief, I wouldn't normally respond to a car accident, but it involved one of my friends from grief group, so I wanted to make sure everything was good.

I was getting ready to head out when the call came through saying there was an accident near Delph Ave, involving a bright green Toyota Corolla. The moment I heard the color, I knew it was Ian. He's the only person in Middleburg that drives a car that color. My mind went into autopilot, and I was grabbing my gear and out the door without making sure I had my phone.

Now that I'm here, I wish I would've waited for more information before racing to the rescue, because this is only a minor fender bender. I could be at lunch with Gwen right now instead of getting information from Ian and the lady who rear-ended him.

I finish collecting the details needed and head back to my car. Looking at the time, I see that I'm now over an hour late. I put the gear in reverse and head straight to Leroy's, praying she's still there as I drive.

Approaching the restaurant, I notice Gwen's van in the parking lot and let out a sigh of relief that she didn't leave. I pull into the spot next to her and immediately notice she's in her driver's seat with her head leaning down on the steering wheel. Jumping out of my car without even turning off the ignition, I run to her.

"Gwen, are you okay? Are you hurt? What's going on?" I rush out, throwing open the door, examining her body for signs of injury.

Her glassy eyes turn to me, roaming over my body before she crumbles in what looks like relief. Her fingers that were white-knuckling the steering wheel release their hold before she lunges into my arms. "Paul! Oh thank God! Are *you* okay?" She pulls back and runs her hands over my shoulders, her teary eyes inspecting my body.

Nodding my head, I pull her into my embrace again. "I'm good, Babe. What's the matter? Why are you crying? Did something happen to Max . . . or Brandi?"

Her body relaxes into mine as I hold her, vanilla and honey filling my nostrils as I breathe in the scent of her. "Nothing. Everyone's all right . . . Now . . . Everything's all right now. I just—I thought you were in a car accident." Her voice breaks.

Drawing back, I hold her arms so I can look at her. "Why would you think I was in an accident?"

"You were late. I called and texted—I texted Tessa . . . she suggested I call the station—" Hiccups break up her sentence. "Faith said . . . Faith said there was . . . an accident—" Sobs wrack through her body at the word accident.

I guide the two of us up so we're both standing and I wrap my arms around her again. "Shh shh. It's okay. I went on a call for an accident and I left my phone at work. I'm such an idiot; of course you'd be worried. I'm so fucking sorry." Kissing her temple, I mutter another apology.

When she pulls back just enough to look me in the eyes, her gorgeous blues shine bright, but a look of fear still lingers. "I really thought I lost you. All I kept thinking was, I never told you that I love you . . . and that I'd never get the chance to say it."

My breath catches, but it takes my brain a moment to register the words she said.

I love you.

I feel her heartbeat pick up as she silently waits for me to say anything. Instead of verbally responding, I lean forward and kiss her, my mouth trying to convey through our connection exactly how I feel about her.

"I love you, too," I say into her lips as she breaks the kiss. "We agreed long ago we weren't playing any games, so I should've told you the moment I realized it."

Her smile returns, small and soft, as she straightens her body. "Maybe you should turn off your car and we can go have our lunch date?" She wipes at the remaining tears streaking down her face.

Quickly shutting off the car and returning to her side, she reaches for my hand. Walking to the entrance of the restaurant, we spot a cardinal on the bush next to the door. We both go still and watch the bird stare at us—seemingly giving us its blessing—before flying away.

Epilogue
Gwen

1 year later . . .

I'm trying to fight off tears as I adjust Max's collar underneath his graduation gown. He's come a long way since he started at Middleburg High, and it's finally time for him to graduate.

Max swats my hands away from his neck. "Okay, Mom, that's enough." He looks around the bleachers as they begin to fill up. "Is everyone coming?"

"They'll be here. You know how it's been for Tessa and Graham since Sheridan was born. It takes them an extra twenty minutes to get out the door, even if they plan to leave an hour early." I smile thinking about Paul's daughter, son-in-law, and eleven-month-old granddaughter.

"And everyone else?" I catch a small hitch in his voice. His eyes are frantically searching the crowd, looking for someone.

Stepping to the side, I make room for Kyle to move next to Max. I reach over and grab his arm. "Paul will be here. He took off work and told them to call Larry if there's any emergencies that arise. He'll probably ride with Tess."

He visibly relaxes at my answer. "She's right. He'll be here," Kyle says, nudging Max in the shoulder, then pointing to a spot near the top of the risers where I see a few friends from work, Brandi, her current boyfriend, Tessa, and Graham. And standing between Tessa and Brandi—holding a very smiley baby girl—is Paul.

I'm not sure how, but Paul spots us in the crowd and begins to wave his and Sheridan's arms in our direction, causing a grin to break through Max's face. The relationship Max and Paul have built over the last year is one I couldn't have dreamed of. Paul sits up late at night playing video games with Max, he helps him with his homework, he even got Max interested in tossing the football again, and they go out with Graham for *guy days*—whatever those entail. Once Paul told Max he never wanted, or intended to replace Dwayne as his father, a switch flipped within him.

"Okay, Bud, I'm going to go join the crew. We'll be up there cheering loudly. I'm so proud of you." I wrap him in a hug before he's able to push me away in embarrassment. "I love you," I whisper into his ear before stepping back.

Watching the ceremony progress causes me to cry on multiple occasions, the gravity of the event sinking in. *My baby is graduating high school.* He decided he doesn't want to go away for college, and he plans on going to the community college one town over, while living at home. Which I'm okay with, especially since his seizures haven't shown any signs of letting up.

"Holly Vochazer." The recognition that the principal is close to Max's name pulls me back. I clap half-heartedly for the girl walking across the stage.

"Maxwell Waters."

I stand up, hollering and clapping in a fit of excitement. "Whoo! Way to go, Max!" Even from here I can see his cheeks flush.

Calming down, I reach for Sheridan and take my seat. "I'm sorry I was so loud. I'm just so excited for Max. Yes, I am," I say in baby talk, bouncing her on my knees. Her face lights up and she giggles, reaching her chubby hands up to pull on my earrings.

After the ceremony, Max asks to get Leroy's takeout to bring back to the house for his celebration dinner. I offer to go pick it up, but he insists on going with Paul so I catch a ride home with Brandi while Paul takes my car to get the food.

When everyone is back at the house, we settle in the living room and turn on *Jurassic Park*. Max and Tessa sit on the floor, whispering to each other and glancing up at Paul and I who are cuddled on the couch. I stick my tongue out at them when I catch them watching us, causing them to laugh.

"Gwen, I love you," Paul says, and I blink a few times when the movie suddenly stops playing.

I look up at him, confused but smiling. He often tells me he loves me at random times of the day, but I'm not sure why the movie had to stop. Feeling eyes on me, I look around and notice everyone watching, so I sit up and wipe at my face. "Is there something on me?"

"No, you look beautiful," Paul says, grabbing my hand. "Gwen, I never thought, after I lost Sherri, that I would find someone to believe in me—someone to challenge me and make me happy again. Then I met you, and I was scared at how those feelings of uncertainty quickly melted away. I thought that having you in my life so soon after losing my wife meant I was betraying her for moving on so quickly." He takes a breath and wipes a tear from my cheek. "She would have loved you. And knowing that makes this all so much easier. I fell in love with you because of your kind heart and your love for those you care about. I keep falling in love with you because of your resilience, your sense of adventure and your determination. You inspire me to continue following my dreams and I'm so proud of you for following yours and getting yourself a job that brought you back to the type of engineering you wanted to do. Gwen, you've become my best friend, the one I want to share the rest of my tomorrows with. Will you do me the honor of marrying me?"

Tears fall from my eyes as I look from him to a box he pulled out of his pocket sometime during his speech. My eyes find Max before I look back to Paul and see he has a hopeful smile on his face, his head softly nodding as he mouths *"Yes."* Turning my attention back to Paul, I lean in to kiss him and whisper against his mouth, the second easiest yes I've ever said. "I'd be delighted to marry you, *Chief Gunter.*"

Dicktionary

For those who like to know where the spice is, to either avoid or prepare:

Acknowledgements

I'd like to start by thanking my husband for continuing to support me without question, and for encouraging me to follow my dreams of writing these emotional and spicy books. His unwavering love and devotion makes it easy for me to create these dreamy MMC's for each book. I've got a great example in you.

My incredible daughter—the fact that she's watching me and soaking in everything I do only encourages me more. She'll randomly walk up to me and ask "Who's reading your books today, Mommy?" And just knowing that she's supporting me and is by my side keeps me going.

My friends and family, the list of those who know about my writing has grown since I wrote *Falling Apart Together* and you all have been nothing but supportive of me. Thank you for being encouraging and sharing my work with your friends and coworkers, that means the world to me.

My alpha readers, Natalie and Nikki. You two are the real MVPs, reading this when it made little sense and was still ideas being worked through in my brain. You loved the characters and could see my vision from the beginning. Thank you for reading and helping me make tweaks that made it worthy of becoming what it is now.

My beta babes, Nessa Bloom, Kelli Cooke, Mary Di-Marzo, @annalees_reading, Sam Schreiber, @goodgirls-bookshelf, and @johnson.reads for reading *Happy Times Too* and leaving your honest opinions, and telling me when something didn't make sense, or when you had an idea that might take my idea and enhance it. You left your thoughts—the good, the bad, and the funny—all which helped make this novella worth publishing.

My wonderful editor, Caitlin Lengerich, you took my book and polished and edited it until the mistakes were—maybe not non-existent—but pretty damn near close. Working with you might have just started out as an editor/author relationship, but it quickly became a friendship that I cherish, so thank you for both relation-ships.

Those indie author friends—my author group chat ladies, those that have stuck by side from the beginning of this journey, and those I've met along the way. Thank you for allowing me to vent or toss ideas your way, and for always being there, without judgement. I thank you all and wish you all the best on your author journeys as well.

My talented cover artist, Lauren Gnapi with Elemental Opal. Girl, you did it AGAIN! I had a few different visions with possible cover designs and you were able to take one and bring it to life. The colors, the mini golf course, the couple—it's all just perfect. Thank you for your beau-tiful creation!

My street team, we may be a small group of book lovers, but you are all incredible. Thank you for all the support you've given me and for being part of my team and hyping my book babies up.

Lastly, you, my readers. Thank you. Thank you for taking a chance on this indie author and going on the emotional ride that was *Happy Times Too*. Whether this book did what I hoped and allowed you to feel all the emotions—the heartbreak and eventual joy and love that Paul and Gwen felt, or it was just a random read to get you one read closer to your reading goal. I appreciate you for picking it up and reading it. Thank you, and I hope you have a wonderful day.

About the author

Image drawn by @junidraws.ca

J.B. Lee was born and raised in Florida but life brought her to Virginia where she has spent the last decade of her life. J.B. is a wife and mother. When she's not spending time with her husband and daughter she is reading or writing. She started writing in March 2023 when the same scene kept playing out in her mind until she put it down in her notes app. She has since added many story ideas to her notes app in hopes of bringing these characters to life. J.B. has a degree in elementary education and spent six years in the classroom and wants to one day return, but for now she enjoys creating stories that will pull at your heartstrings while also giving you a happily ever after.

Also by J.B. Lee
Falling Apart Together